For my Father

Then the LORD God said, "Behold, the man has become like one of us in knowing good and evil. Now, lest he reach out his hand and take also of the Tree of Life and eat, and live forever—"

- Genesis 3:22

… To the one who conquers I will grant to eat of the Tree of Life, which is in the paradise of God.'

- Revelation 2:7b

CHAPTER ONE

"This is a drag," grumbled Kurt to the other guys, trying to be cool enough by not being too loud about it, but with enough emphasis that someone would hear. He kicked at a few stones next to what once was a stream or riverbed but dried up long ago under California's hot sun. Thousands of rocks formed a path through the countryside; softly polished, they were great for skipping along the water at the lake. He absently wiped sweat from his freckled brow and swatted at a cloud of gnats before grabbing a couple more rocks and stuffing them in his pocket.

"Your dad is the one who set this up," shot back Alan. "To make bonds with each other to last a lifetime... blah, blah, blah..." Alan rolled his hands in gestures to signify the hypocrisy of it all. Alan was the class clown. Not so much as to get into trouble, but he always had a comeback for every situation. His wavy blond hair reached his shoulders although the top of his head barely made it past Kurt's shoulder.

"Hey! Let's just get the rocks we need and get back to camp."

1

Kurt said.

Kurt wanted to get ammunition for his new slingshot he ordered and get a chance to use it. The other two guys were doing the same thing, looking for the perfect shaped rocks to fit into the leather strap to be pulled back. Too big, it won't go that far. Too sm

all, won't cause enough damage.

There were three of them, and they had been practically inseparable since elementary school. Kurt, the tallest, was the ringleader. He was also the oldest who just turned thirteen. The other two were twelve. They grew up together in Southern California, but presently they were camping a bit north outside of San Diego County at Indian Wells Campgrounds. They went back to hunting for the perfect shaped rocks while the sun drifted across the summer blue sky, Terence barely exaggerating his limp from the charley horse Alan gave him earlier that day on a bet.

With their pockets full, they trudged off again towards camp, which was to the south on the other side of an old unused barn with a rickety wooden fence around it. The fence was knocked down in many areas, but had a few stable ledges they could place targets on. It was also painted white, which would make the targets easier to see.

Terence suggested, "Hey, let's shoot a few of these rocks before we get back to camp." The others thought it was a great idea. So, they hunted around for objects they could line up on the fence and pick off with their slingshots—trash left behind by previous campers who didn't care about the area, a couple of soda cans, and a boot, not a cowboy boot, more like a military boot.

Both Terence and Alan pulled back their elastic band and let a rock fly. One rock missed its target completely, but the other one ricocheted off the heel of the boot and dropped to the ground, barely moving the object.

"That was mine," piped in Terence. "I hit it."

"No, I was aiming at the boot," said Alan.

"OK, each one of ya, take your turn on the boot and see who can knock it off first," commanded Kurt. "Then I'll use my new slingshot and show you guys how it's all done."

Terence lined up first. The sound of the rock skittering off the fence post was enough to know he didn't land his shot.

Kurt noted the sun dipping lower in the southwestern sky, and the shadows getting quite long. With the color of the river rocks, finding them might be a little hard to do if they let the light get away from them.

Alan lined up and brandished his slingshot. He bought it from an out-of-state store his dad took him to on their last vacation back east. The chrome was still shiny, and the rubber hadn't darkened that much yet. He pulled back his shot and took aim, somewhere in the middle of the Y-shape held in his left hand. He let go, and a second later, one of the soda cans flew off the fence.

"I meant to do that," Alan said, brandishing his fist in a power play motion.

"Sure, you did," grumbled Terence.

"Did too!" he emphasized, "I wasn't aiming for that stupid boot. These rocks aren't heavy enough to knock that thing down. That boot is huge."

Kurt reached down into his pocket. He felt around for the perfect stone and found it. This one felt very round. It didn't have the heft of the other rocks, but he figured it'd make up for it in less drag for the shape. He put it in the brand-new leather strap of his slingshot and pulled back, taking aim at the center of the boot. He was a pretty good shot most of the time, but this was a big boot. Knocking that thing off would be tricky. The other boys couldn't hide their admiration at his new weapon. It was jet black, except for the elastic. It had chrome highlights at the connections, and intricate blue lettering of the name of the company going down the arm brace.

"Whoa! When did you pick that one up?" asked Alan.

"Is that a Rocket MTX-3?" asked Terence.

"No," Kurt said and pulled back the strap. "It's the MTX-4 that came out two months ago that I've been saving for all summer."

When Kurt let go of the strap, the rock launched toward the boot. A slight trail of green light shimmered off the rock as it flew through the air. The boys were speechless as they watched the rock hit the boot and go straight through it! The rock continued into the barn, plowed a hole the same size in the wood, with a wisp of smoke emitting from the edges of the hole. There was a knock, kind of like the sound you hear when you play billiards and shoot the cue ball into the other balls, and then nothing.

The boys froze. They looked at each other, then at the holes, at each other again. Alan was the first to speak, "Awesome wrist-rocket, Kurt!"

"What?" asked Kurt. He was dazed thinking about what happened. He shot a few rocks with his gear before, but nothing like this ever happened. "Wait. That wasn't the slingshot. That was the rock."

Before he could get the words all the way out of his mouth, the other boys scampered towards the boot to see what kind of damage was caused—a clear hole outlined through the leather like it was tissue paper. With a brief pause, they stopped to see, then continued to the barn to go look for the stone.

Kurt trailed behind, still trying to work things out. When he reached the boot, he stuck his finger through one side and another finger through the other, touching fingertips in the middle. The edges of the hole were warm as if it burned its way through. He lumbered on to the barn to catch up with the other two.

They took tentative steps towards the open door, barely hanging on by its hinges. The place had been ransacked a dozen times over. Graffiti was sprayed on the exterior marking various local gangs and logos, and general nonsense.

With the sun setting below the edge of the mountains, it was getting a little darker now, and the shadows inside the barn were unfriendly at best. Once inside, it wasn't hard to track down where the rock had gone. The last trickle of daylight shone through the hole created by the stone, along with a multitude of other compromises in the barn's structure to give a little light into the center of the area.

There were stables inside with thick wooden doors and walls, each having a similar hole in it, but at the same level with no drop because of gravity. It even put a hole through the metal latch that held one of the doors closed! Alan lined up close to where the stone entered the barn and looked through all the holes but just saw darkness after a few yards. He pulled out his keychain, which had a laser light he used to torture his cat, and held it to the hole. The light streamed through several holes, finally ending on a sign in one of the stables.

Going to that stable area, the boys pushed around the straw a bit until Kurt found his rock again. It apparently hit a granite plaque that was hanging on the back of the stall with the previous occupant's name engraved upon it, before it fell to the ground.

All three ran back outside so they could get a better look at their find.

Kurt yelled to the other guys, "Hey! Check this out!" The stone was slightly darker than the other stones they used, but that wasn't the big deal. It looked like it was a perfect sphere. River rocks tended to have elongated shapes, even though they were very smooth, but this one was in a sphere. He had bored the other kids with his ideas of aerodynamics and physics of rocks flying in the air on the walk over. "You see? A perfect sphere has no drag. You can launch this puppy and it'll shoot straight as an arrow."

Terence piped in, "That's just a marble."

"No, it's not! See the texture? It's not glassy like a marble," responded Kurt, "it's more like the texture of a stone, but not quite."

"What do you mean, 'not quite'?" asked Alan.

"I mean it looks and feels like a rock, but it seems lighter than it should for its size. Check this out." Kurt handed it to Terence first.

When Terence took a hold of the rock, he dropped it right away. "Yikes, that's sharp!" he said. Blood was clearly dripping from his fingers. He winced as he grabbed his bloody palm with his other hand. "What the..."

"No way, it's perfectly smooth," answered back Kurt. Kurt picked the stone back up again and rubbed it back and forth between his fingers and palms. "See? There aren't any sharp edges. Maybe you just had something sharp in your hand already. Try again."

"No, thanks," said Terence. "I'm not touching that thing. Alan, you touch it."

"Ok, wussy," Alan put his hand out with confidence.

Kurt dropped the stone into Alan's waiting palm and just as it touched his skin, Alan's hand felt like it was bursting into flames. He reflexively pulled his hand out from under it and let it drop to the ground.

"Jeez! That thing is on fire!" exclaimed Alan. "How can you carry it?"

"I don't know," Kurt answered back, easily picking up the stone between finger and thumb off the ground and looking at it closely, once again noticing it felt lighter than it looked.

"That thing must be cursed or something," Terence suggested.

"Yeah, and you're still bleeding!"

Terence looked down at his hands just as another drop of blood made its way to the corner of his palm and fell to the ground. He quickly wrapped it up in his shirt and played like it wasn't a big deal.

Kurt nodded and put the rock back in his pocket. "Don't tell anyone about this rock. I want to find out more about it, and if anyone knows, they'll take it away from us."

"You mean take it away from you," Alan corrected.

"No, us," Kurt reiterated. "We're the ones who found it together. We're the team." They were too old for the games they used to play where they were part of a secret brotherhood or club, but they still had that certain comradery that kids have when they have been together for many years. "This is ours to handle. I'll hold on to it for now until we figure out how someone else can hold it too, but it belongs to all of us. Now just play cool when we get back to camp."

Kurt put his fist in the middle of them, and each in turn put their fists in as well, signifying that what was said there was going to be only for them to know. They turned, and started heading back for the campgrounds, each of them wondering about the day's events, while the last sliver of sunlight ducked behind the far-off peaks.

By the time the kids returned, there was a fire going that was probably a bit larger than needed, considering they weren't using it to cook any food. Alan's dad had his portable hot plate plugged into the gas-powered generator in the bed of his GMC truck and was stirring away while the boys found empty seats to sit around and get warm. It smelled like they broke out the "gourmet" pork 'n beans from the ninety-nine-cent store, with a heavy molasses odor.

"About time you boys showed up," said Mr. Palmer, Kurt's dad. "We were about to go hunting for you." The other boys probably thought Mr. Palmer was playing around, but Kurt knew how serious his dad was being. Ever since he was younger, after his mom died, his dad had been very protective of him. Not having any siblings, it was just the two of them, and they leaned on each other. Kurt could see his dad relax knowing his son was nearby. His mom's death had taken quite a toll on his dad, and he never spoke about it. When he would ask about it, his dad would try to change the subject or downplay the issue—never a straight answer. He knew it was some type of mental disease or dementia that had taken her early, but the process was just too hard for his dad to talk about, and he never pushed much for more information.

Kurt leaned forward and grabbed a soda from the ice chest. He grabbed a few more and tossed them to his other friends, getting a chuckle when they splashed a little when opened. Mr. Watson came around, handing out the beans and franks in generic paper bowls to each person. With a flourish, he would hand them a napkin and a plastic fork as well.

"Dad! Beans again?" Alan asked. "This is the third time this week we've had beans."

"By no means, again!" his dad snapped back with a grin. "We had lentils last night, frijoles the night before that, and tonight it's beans and franks—completely different things." Alan slapped his face while everyone else snickered. "And tomorrow night, I promise, nothing but the finest legumes."

"That's it, Bobby," said Mr. Jackson, Terence's dad, "stop teasing him. We'll be leaving before tomorrow night and we'll be saved from another night of your attack on our bowels."

"Hey, if someone else wants to cook, I'm all for it," responded Mr. Watson. "Does anyone else have a stove they'd like to bring out?" Everyone knew Bobby would always be the cook—it's just what he did when all of them came out camping. But everyone liked to get their jabs in occasionally, just for fun.

Mr. Jackson, Terence's dad, asked, "Well, what were you boys up to?"

Furtive looks went around for a moment before Kurt spoke up. "We were just looking around for stuff. You know, arrowheads, and things." The campgrounds were part of the native American reservation, and they had found a broken arrowhead a couple of years back when they had camped there before. The site had been long picked over now.

"Any luck?"

"No," Alan responded, "but we found what looked like a stream of rocks a couple of miles over there," pointing to where they had come from earlier. Kurt passed him a decisive scowl and Alan quickly amended, "but it was boring, so we just came back." It sounded natural enough not to bring attention from the surrounding dads. They knew almost everything was boring to the boys nowadays that didn't involve some form of a video game.

Kurt's dad shook his head, "You guys will get your phones back tomorrow in the afternoon when we leave, so you'll be able to return to the vegetative state you once had before this trip began." He didn't understand why these kids spent so much time with their faces glued to these phones. He had only gotten a smartphone this past year because there weren't any other options available. "A phone is a phone," he would tell Kurt, "and a computer is a computer, and never the twain shall meet in my pocket." Kurt would always crack back about how old his dad was and how it must have been awful scraping dinosaur poop from his shoes when he got home from the one-room schoolhouse after walking twelve miles in the snow, uphill, both ways. "Time to call it a night. But, before we do, didn't you hear something on the radio earlier Bobby?"

"Why yes, everyone, grab your drinks and huddle in close to the fire. I've got something to tell you about..."

Bobby was the best at telling ghost stories. He always made them seem like they were news reports or things he read on the internet that were factual. The boys would be on the edge of their seats, not noticing that Terence's dad had snuck out for the coup de grâce at the end of the storytelling. There was a guarantee of shock value, but all in good fun. At least Terence wouldn't cry this time like he did a couple of years ago, or so they hoped.

After the stories were done, they packed their stuff away and entered the tents for the night's sleep. The sound of crickets was deafening, only counterpointed by the croaking of toads at the lake. The breeze was cooling down, and the boys snuggled into their sleeping bags without complaint. The lake was a good fifty yards away at least, but the slight smell of still water was evident. It held the promise of fishing in the morning, something the boys loved to do. Who could resist that smell of jarred salmon eggs, freshly opened, or that stink cheese for the catfish? It didn't take long for all of them to fall fast asleep.

* * *

Kurt's forgotten dream was always the same:

...After the last pair of animals walked onto the Ark, God reached out and sealed the door. Everything would be blotted out, so God ordered his chief angels to fly down to Eden and remove the Tree of Life. The rain had already begun, and since it never rained before, the masses of people were scared and ran to take cover, not noticing the flashing lights in the sky as the angels passed over.

Seven Archangels were required to accomplish such a task—Gabriel, Michael, Raphael, Chamuel, Jophiel, Ariel, and Azrael. They landed at the edge of the Garden of Eden where the Cherubim guarded the path to the Tree..

CHAPTER TWO

A tinny sounding Eye of the Tiger chorus broke the silence in the morning, just as the sun was lightening the sky in the east. Alan's dad rolled over and absently pressed the screen on his phone to turn it off. Everyone was slowly starting to move, anxious for the new day. With fishing on the itinerary, the motivation was in earnest to get going to the lake. They packed up their tents and gear they wouldn't need for the rest of the day, so when it was time to finish, they could head straight to the road.

By the time the group got down to the water's edge, there wasn't any of the misty fog left behind that they had seen a couple of the other mornings. The lake expanded in both directions with a meandering of paths and they could barely see the pier and tackle shop from where they were settling in. They had all the things they needed to catch the likely hauls of trout, bass, or catfish. There was a thick vegetation of green algae lining the lake which stretched out about five feet or so. The dads reminded the kids when they were pulling their lines in, to try to keep it from pulling through the muck or they'd just lose their bait every time.

After a couple of hours, the boys started getting fidgety. The fish weren't biting and the attention span of a teen or pre-teen does not accommodate the finer mastery of the rod and reel. Terence leaned over to Kurt and whispered, "Maybe there might be more?" He gestured to Kurt's pocket, trying not to draw attention. Kurt looked back at him with awe. He didn't think of that. He was so occupied by what happened yesterday that it didn't cross his mind that there might be other stones like the one they had already found.

"Alright," Kurt answered back, "let me handle it."

Kurt walked over to his dad and talked quietly to him for a few minutes. Everyone kept silent so they wouldn't startle the fish. His dad looked a bit disappointed but gave a slight nod. Walking towards his friends, Kurt gestured them to huddle up.

"Ok, guys, my dad said we can do some more exploring. When he asked about us saying it was boring, I told him it couldn't be more boring than sitting here for two hours doing nothing. We just have to be back by noon to get ready to go."

The boys started off towards the area they found the special rock the day before. It took them a good thirty minutes to walk there, so they knew they didn't have a lot of time to search around.

When they finally arrived, Kurt spoke up, "Let's split up since we don't have a lot of time. I'll look around where I found the rock yesterday. Terence, head over that way and Alan, you go the opposite direction. We'll meet up back here in twenty minutes. Don't go too far off because the riverbed's turns and banks cut the line of sight. After a couple of turns, we won't be able to hear each other."

"Got it," said Alan, "but I'm not touching anything. I'll mark anything I find, and you can pick it up when we meet up again."

"Good idea," said Kurt. "Terence, don't touch anything. Just put a stick in the ground near any rock you think looks like this one."

Kurt looked closely around the area he thought he found the rock before. As far as he could see, all the rocks were the elliptical-shaped river rocks. Here and there, he'd see a broken piece of granite, quartz, or limestone, but nothing that resembled the unique aspects of the rock he'd found yesterday. He brought the rock out again to look at it. It didn't have a chip or mark from hitting the granite plate in the barn, so he figured it must be tough, but it didn't feel that heavy. It felt as though the surface were somewhat porous, but no holes were evident. There really wasn't anything to distinguish it from any other rock of its size or shape.

He finally gave up searching for another of its kind and called out to his friends. He could hear responses from either side and see Alan running toward him. When he joined him, he asked, "Did you find anything?"

"No," and Alan continued, "nothing even close to that shape. Hey, where's Terence?"

"C'mon, let's go get him. It's getting close to time to leave."

The pair headed northeast along the dried-up riverbed in the direction Terence had gone. It didn't take them more than a few minutes to see what was holding him up. Ahead about fifty feet, where a sharp bend in the river's course happened with a tall bank, Terence was backed up against the protruding granite rocks lining the side of the wash. His hands and arms were tucked into his body tightly, making himself the smallest target for what might be causing his angst. The blue baseball cap he wore all the time was a few feet away from him in the dirt, showing his natural hair that probably hadn't been picked out all week.

The boys walked closer, trying to call out to Terence, but his eyes just got wider in fear. About thirty feet away, they could see, and hear, what was causing it, a western rattlesnake. Kurt motioned Alan to stay still where they were. He softly spoke into his ear, "People used to think that snakes couldn't hear because they didn't have ears, but they can, so keep quiet. If that snake gets anxious, he could bite Terence. I'm going to make a sound behind the snake with my sling-shot so it'll distract the snake and he can get out of there."

Kurt crept closer, watching his footing so he wouldn't make any extra sounds. When he was about twenty feet away, he slowly pulled out his weapon and the special rock he'd found. He remembered how loud the noise was when the rock hit the granite nameplate, so he was hoping for the same now. He aimed just over and behind the snake to get him to move back, pulled the elastic, and let it fly.

The snake noticed Kurt's movement or saw the green flare of the rock and instinctively tried to bite at Terence. Kurt felt horror as he looked at his friend and the snake going toward him. Just as he did, the stone curved its path mid-air and aimed straight at the snake in mid-flight, its green fiery trail growing larger. When the stone reached the snake, it obliterated the head in flames. The stone continued until it hit the granite boulder behind and fell to the ground. Kurt ran over to make sure Terence was OK, Alan trailing behind him.

"That was some nice shooting," Terence said.

"No, that wasn't me. That was the rock," responded Kurt, while picking it up and looking at it again - no marks, no chips, and no blood on it either. He put it back in his pocket, thankful, but still wondering what this thing was all about. "Let's get going, we're going to be late if we don't hurry."

A couple of excuses for being late and a couple of hours later, and they were back on the road heading south.

* * *

Kurt's forgotten dream was always the same:

...The Archangels landed at the edge of the Garden of Eden where the Cherubim guarded the path to the Tree. Gabriel motioned to the lesser angel who knew by the arrival of the supreme class of angels that his job was complete. As the Cherubim left, Gabriel's eyes locked onto the target of his mission. Flanked by his six brothers, they walked the few hundred cubits to the tree, marveling at its size and complexities. Twelve different fruits of various size and color, yet all perfectly consistent, grew from its branches amid the emerald of its leaves whose touch could heal wounds. The angels encircled the trunk, enjoying the warmth and life it provided...

Stone of Gabriel

CHAPTER THREE

T he families had returned from camp only two weeks before school started again. Kurt always carried the stone around as a lucky piece—he even found a way to braid a string around it to keep it around his neck so he wouldn't lose it. He and his friends were so busy with getting backpacks, notebooks, orientations for eighth grade, and more, the things that happened at camp seemed to drift into the background.

Kurt, Terence, and Alan lived in the same apartment complex in El Cajon, California, a city in the central-eastern part of San Diego County. There weren't many places to use a slingshot in town, so there wasn't much to do with the rock except try to guess about its nature. When they were done with homework after school, the three boys would get together to hang out in the pool room in the middle of the apartment complex and try to figure things out. They would get their phones out and try to search for similar objects online. Kurt pulled the list out of his apps of what they had tried so far.

"Maybe it's nuclear?" suggested Alan.

"I'm not sure, but I think we'd all be sick by now," responded Kurt. He entered that on the list and put a mark through it. Some items had question marks, like a meteorite, stone giant's eyeball, and very old marble. The rest had lines through them signifying they didn't think that was the case.

"We could talk to Mr. Ferguson. He's really cool," Terence said. Mr. Ferguson was the science teacher and he performed all kinds of experiments in class to show how things react together.

"Not yet," answered Kurt, "as soon as we talk to an adult about this, we'll get it taken away from us. This is still our find."

"I wonder why you can hold it, and nothing happens to you, but when we hold it, it's always bad," mumbled Terence.

"Well, here," Kurt said, "put your hand in your jacket pocket and try to touch it. See what happens."

Kurt took off the chain and dangled it in front of himself waiting for Terence to take it. Terence squinted his eyes closed, getting ready to feel the pain again, like the shock you expect when you rub your feet on the carpet and touch metal. He put his clothed hand around it and held it. Nothing happened.

"Cool!" Terence said.

"OK, so we know you can handle it in an emergency, just don't touch it directly." Kurt put the necklace back on.

Some other teens in the complex ambled in the door to play billiards, so Kurt closed the app. They could talk about it later.

The news was playing on the screen in the pool room, the volume turned down and the closed captions flitted across the bottom. Kurt glanced at the TV while they showed a man being taken in handcuffs by the police. He was fighting against the officers and they had to restrain him with zip ties. When his face peeked through his unruly hair, Kurt saw something strange—the face was contorted in a way that was unnatural, the eyes solid red. "Hey, did you see that?" Kurt asked.

"Yeah, that guy was wrestling all over the place. They had three or four cops loading him into that car," answered Alan.

"No, did you see how weird his face looked and those eyes?" Kurt asked.

Alan responded, "What about them? He looked pissed, but normal enough, what did you see?"

"Never mind. Hey, c'mon." Kurt gestured they should follow him. He walked them a few dozen yards away, pulled out the key to his house, and opened the door.

Kurt escorted them inside and said, "Guys, sit on the couch while I try to get that show back on the TV so you can see what I was talking about. Pay close attention to his face this time."

He tried to get the channel back on his TV after closing the door. It was on a different news channel, but they said the same story was about to be coming up.

Kurt looked and saw the same unnatural facial expression and red eyes. He pointed at the screen this time, "You see that? Do you see the red eyes?"

"No, his eyes aren't red," said Terence while Alan backed him up shaking his head.

Alan came up with an idea, "Kurt, take off the stone."

Kurt lifted his hands and took the chain from his neck and put it on the coffee table. He looked back at the TV. "What the heck? He looks normal now!"

Alan, feeling curious, leaned his hand over to the coffee table and lightly pressed his fingertip to the stone while looking at the screen. When he made contact, his fingertip felt like it was bursting into flames, but nothing changed on the screen. He yanked his hand back and clutched his finger.

"What'd you do?" asked Terence.

"The damn thing burned me!" Alan yelled. He looked at Kurt, "But I didn't see anything like you were talking about. The guy on TV still looked the same."

Kurt put his chain back around his neck. "Great. Now I'm seeing things."

"Maybe it's because you're not hurt by the stone," suggested Terence, "somehow it likes you...or knows you. Maybe it only works with you."

"But why me?" asked Kurt. "Anyway, do you think I should let them know that guy isn't what he appears to be?"

"Yeah, right," laughed Terence, "like they'd believe you. I know you and I have a hard time believing you."

"Yeah, you're probably right," Kurt half-heartedly laughed along. But he still had a strange feeling about that man or thing or whatever he was. If he didn't tell someone about it, somebody could get hurt, and that would be on him.

* * *

"Hey, Steve!" called out Rudy with the phone clamped to his shoulder, "there's a kid on the line that says your last catch isn't human. What?" He listened to the phone again, "Make that a kid faking like he's an adult says your last catch isn't human," Rudy barely got through laughing.

Steve didn't seem as amused. He walked over to his desk, opposite Rudy's, and picked up his line. He put the phone to his ear and motioned the call transfer. while sitting down. "This is Detective

Bailey. What kind of game is going on?"

"Not a game, sir. I just wanted to let someone know that when I saw Barry Finley on TV getting arrested, he didn't look completely human. He might be an alien or something because I saw his eyes turn red and his face was a different shape," said in a voice that sounded like a young teenager.

"Look, kid. You've been watching too many science fiction movies or something," Steve placated back to him. "Let me get your name and number, and I'll let you know if something comes up of it."

"No, sir, I don't want to get involved. I just wanted to let someone know about it. I'm sorry to have bothered you. Goodbye." There was a quick click on the line, and it was dead.

Steve pulled the handset away from his face with a dumbfounded look, "Crazy kids these days. Too much imagination," and put the phone down. Rudy just hmphed and went back to his computer screen. Steve looked up at the clock, noted he still had an hour on the shift, and got up. "I have to check up on some things in property and question Finley. If any more kids want to talk to me, you handle it."

Detective Bailey walked down the hall, stopping by reception first to ask, "Hey, I just had a call at my desk. Do me a favor and trace that call and send it to my phone." The uniformed officer gave him the thumbs up, and he kept walking to the interrogation rooms where he had left Finley earlier to stew. He put his hand on the doorknob to the viewing room next to Finley's, took a breath, and walked in.

Steve had picked this specific room because no one else cared for it much. Most of the other viewing rooms were positioned higher in reference to the interrogation room for a better perspective. This viewing room was just a dark room made of cinder blocks at an equal level to interrogation room four. The dim light coming through the two-way mirror was kept bright on the other side. There was a black cable coming from the ceiling down to the window and along the side with a switch and a microphone/speaker apparatus for talking into the next chamber. The video monitor set in the wall was the old CRT model, black and white, low contrast. Steve looked through the glass at Barry Finley, trying to decide what to ask next. Barry's hair was wavy in wet locks like he'd been sweating for hours in the sun, although the room was air-conditioned. There weren't the usual handcuffs of a somewhat compliant suspect—this guy took four officers to bring down. Although he didn't look that large compared to Steve's six-foot two-inch frame, his strength was off the charts. The other officers figured he was worked up on street drugs to generate that much aggression. His hands were balled on the table, with cuffs and chains at the wrist, elbow, midsection, and legs. The cuffs on his hands were run through a bolted mass of steel on the table, and his foot cuffs were chained similarly to the ground. There was no way this get-up was comfortable in the least, but he just sat there with his head tilted down, black mass of hair covering his face, and deeply breathing as if he were getting ready to jump.

Steve waited for a time, then reached his hand up to the microphone switch. Instead of clicking it on to make himself heard, he ran his hand behind the speaker and pulled out the audio lines. Then he left the small bunker and entered the room with Barry Finley. Unlike the last time, he skirted the room, reached for the folding chair, stood up on it, and pulled the wire from the video camera in the room. Finley didn't make a move. Steve grabbed the chair and pulled it up to the table in front of Finley, placing some files on the metal table between them. About that time, he noticed his phone was buzzing with the address of the caller he requested from the receptionist earlier. He contemplated and concluded that there might be more pressing issues than dealing with this scum.

"I don't have much time…" Steve began.

"You sure don't," came the riposte from inside the hairy mass. His voice sounded like dry rustling leaves. Even being prepared for the sound, it was unsettling. Steve wasn't afraid. He couldn't remember the last time he'd been afraid. Finley slowly lifted his head menacingly. As soon as he looked up, Steve could see the red eyes staring back at him. The twisted features were barely human, but that evil smile would normally send chills down most people's backs.

"Look, just give me the information I want to know, and we'll call it a day," Steve bartered.

"The information you need to know is that I will rend every inch of your skin from your bones," cackled Finley. "I know you, Stephen Michael Bailey."

OK, that's it, thought Steve. He didn't have time to spend with this character. He had been following him for a few days, trying to get a bead on what he was up to, but a couple of rookies had showed up at the wrong time and they had to make an arrest bringing him in. Steve was more interested in what the game was in the bigger picture. "This is going to hurt, a lot…" Thank goodness these rooms were soundproofed. Steve leaned over and placed his hands on the heavily tattooed forearms of Barry.

A guttural raging cry came from Barry's mouth. Where Steve's hands touched him, it appeared like steam or smoke was curling around the edges of his hands. A dull red glow peered through the top of his shirt. Barry's cry became a wet popping noise, and then hundreds of black flying insects came from his throat, twisted black abominations that didn't resemble anything Steve had seen before and called a bug. Ichor dripped from one side of his mouth and then from his nose until the swarm billowed above his body and then flew through the only vent in the room. When the swarm was gone, Barry lay back in his seat only semi-conscious. A small scar that ran from the corner of his eye to his left ear slowly faded. What appeared to be a defensive wound on his right hand also closed and healed over, showing no mark in its absence.

Bailey pulled a handkerchief from his pocket and handed it over to the now complacent suspect. He got up, reattached the video cable, and sat back down. "Mr. Finley, you were telling me why you attacked that family in their home?"

Groggily, Barry started, "Wh-what? What's going on? Hey man, what the hell is going on? Who are you?"

Steve acted as though he were losing his patience, "C'mon bub, don't play stupid now. You were caught coming out of the Connor's house, you dropped a knife next to the stairs, and ran away. You were picked up less than two blocks away from the scene, and just a few minutes ago you were starting to tell me about how it all went down."

Barry's eyes widened but looked pleading. "I…. I… I remember doing all of that, but it wasn't me. It was like I was watching my body do it all."

Steve stood up calmly, gathering his folders. "That's enough for me. Thank you. I'll have another officer in here to take your statement." He opened the door while Barry was yelling behind him to wait, but he just shut it, went into the other room and reattached the speaker wire. He checked to make sure the video feed caught everything he just had recorded and walked back out. To one of the other officers, he said, "Mr. Finley is ready to talk about what he did. He confessed on video. Get the rest of his statement. I have a few things to do." The other officer nodded, grabbed a long yellow pad of paper and pencil, his coffee mug, and walked towards room four. Steve continued down the hall. He knew he had to investigate this caller who could see the same thing he could. This could be a game changer and he didn't have all the facts—he hated not having all the facts.

CHAPTER FOUR

D ays later, the trio were walking home from school and the topic of the stone came up again.

"What if the only thing you can do with it is shoot it from a slingshot? Maybe that's it?" suggested Alan.

"I hope not," returned Kurt, "If that's the case, and I aim it at something and miss, I could lose it. Or, if I hit what I'm aiming at, I could still lose it. Remember that boot? If it didn't hit that sign in the barn, I might have never found it."

"Yeah, I wouldn't be using it regularly as slingshot ammo," volunteered Terence. "Did you try rubbing it and asking for three wishes?" he joked.

"No way," Kurt responded, hoping he came across seriously. In fact, he had tried that the night before on a whim. "It's not a lamp, it's a stone. Don't be stupid."

Kaden's Market was up ahead, a small grocery store that had a bakery, butcher, and a small selection of stand-up video games. They decided to stop by to see if there were any new games since their last visit, since they changed at least one of them out weekly. Even though they all had game consoles at home, there was always the unique feel of an upright game, with controls specifically designed for only that game.

Nearing the entrance, they could smell the fresh-baked goods emitting from the ovens and hear the bustle of employees and pans. A quick look to the left and through the glass, bakers were flipping and spinning dough into different shapes. Some were being made into conchas, sweet Mexican breads which were very popular and colorful. Others were being molded into cemitas, Mexican style rolls. It was mesmerizing to stare at them skillfully about their trade, item after item, carefully placed on long baking sheets before being sent to the ovens. Scents of cinnamon and powdered sugar filled the entrance hallway.

They continued past the customer service booth to the alcove on the right where the video games were. There was a TV playing in the booth and a bored employee absently watched the news with a "Next Teller" sign in front of him, apparently on his break. Terence pulled a quarter out of his pocket and stuck it into the first game while Alan and Kurt watched on. It was Dragon's Fare, a retro-laser-disc game they hadn't seen before.

Alan turned and said, "I'm going to get some candy, I'll be right back," and started to walk off. He took a few steps, then turned around and came back to Kurt, hurriedly. "Hey Kurt, check it out! Your red-eyed monster is on TV again." Kurt scowled at him but followed leaving Terence at the game. Only after a few steps, Kurt could make out the court scene on the TV, with the TV news anchor describing the events.

Kurt asked if the employee could turn it up a little. He did. "…

and at the top of the local news, the alleged multiple-count murderer Barry Finley has pleaded not guilty by reason of insanity." Barry's hair was combed back into a ponytail, but he still had an orange jumpsuit on for the arraignment. He wore glasses now, most likely for the sympathy angle, and carried himself like a shell of the former attack dog he'd shown when multiple officers had to take him down to bring him to custody. What boggled Kurt's mind was that Finley's face appeared completely normal, and Kurt had the Stone around his neck under his shirt and jacket.

Alan whispered, "You see anything?"

"No," answered Kurt, "he looks normal."

"Normal? He's a lunatic!" offered the employee in a clipped accent, "Have you heard about what he did to that family? They say if you see the pictures, you can't go to sleep without nightmares, and that includes adults. He's one with the devil." The employee made the symbol of the cross with his fingers protecting himself from the evils of the world.

The two of them walked back to the video games and filled Terence in on the news.

"So, either you've changed, or he has," said Terence, as if he were stating something profound.

"Uh…duh," shot back Alan, "You think?" with a mocking overbite and crossed eyes. Terence pushed him, but not seriously. They laughed.

"I'm going to see if I can find out anything about Finley online," said Kurt, "You guys coming or staying?" Kurt could look it up on his smartphone, but his dad told him not to use data away from the house, so he needed to be near free Wi-fi.

"I still have five quarters left," said Terence. Alan pulled his hand out of his pocket and brandished a good handful.

"OK, I'll catch up with you guys later," said Kurt as he left. He walked past the bakery, this time with so many questions on his mind, he didn't notice the flour flying. He turned left out the door and jaywalked across Main Street and down to the street he lived on, Oak Glen Road. Nearing his apartment complex, he saw a car parked across the street he had seen the day before when the three of them were walking home. The same guy was sitting in the driver's seat, looking like he was reading a book under the shade of a large elm tree, the shadows from the tree cloaking his entire black sedan.

He was about thirty feet from his complex, across the street from the car, when he heard the man in the seat yell, "Hey, kid. Come over here. I have a question." Kurt turned his head to look at the guy. He had never seen him before. Even sitting down, it was obvious the man was tall, his brown hair barely seen inside the top of the car. He looked simple enough, clean shaven except for a mustache, but his eyes looked like they had seen everything. They were hawkish, and pale blue–he could see from a dozen yards away.

Kurt didn't stop. He had been told by his dad never to speak to strangers. Although he was tall for his age, he wasn't stupid enough to think he could defend himself against an adult toe to toe. He did what he was supposed to do--he ran. He didn't stop until he was at his front door, pulling the key from his pocket, opening the door and gently pressing it behind him and fastening the deadbolt. Normally, he wouldn't have run, but he felt as though this stranger might be stalking him. He stopped and could feel his heart beating in his chest like he'd run a mile. He waited for minutes that felt like hours and dared a look through the peephole in the door. He saw nothing but the front gate of his patio enclosure, a five-foot-tall dark brown fence that surrounded a five-foot by ten-foot-area that apartment renters get to think of as a backyard, except it's in front of their home and paved with concrete. His bike he hadn't ridden for the past month was gathering cobwebs off to the side. He waited for another five minutes before relaxing.

He put his backpack on the table, sat down, and tried to get his mind off things. He turned on the monitor to his computer and started the desktop with a reach down of his left hand. His dad's laptop was across the table, closed. So much for a dining table, he thought. This was their workspace, as they usually had their meals on the coffee table in front of the TV in the living room. It was quiet in the home except for the clicking of the hard drive needle and occasionally the computer fan blowing. Kurt stood up and turned on the TV for some background noise, then went back to the computer.

The monitor was showing the search engine main screen and Kurt entered Barry Finley in the box. Immediately, references to the suspect filled the screen from the various news stations. He clicked on the first one and watched the same clip he had seen earlier at Kaden's Market. He hit the back button and selected another. This one had a few pictures but described the apprehension of Finley by Detective Bailey and a couple of beat officers. It mentioned how many police officers it took to handle the suspect into custody and the alleged crime committed in somewhat redacted detail. Kurt wondered why some people did such horrible things.

He clicked on another link which had an interview with neighbors who lived near Barry before the incident. "He kept to himself a lot, but he didn't make any trouble in the neighborhood," said one of the people in his community.

"He played his heavy metal music too loudly, and I had to call the police a couple of times," said another, while a third nodded. "But after that, there wasn't a problem."

The scene switched to the front driveway of Finley's house,

where the field reporter was speaking in front of the yellow caution tape wrapped around the gate of the house. "Here, the police are searching for additional evidence to tie Barry Finley to the murder of the Connor family. I have one of the police officers here, Officer Jacobs, who is a part of the search. Sir, could you talk a little about what's going on?"

"Not a lot," responded the officer, "This is an ongoing investigation, so information regarding this case is not available to the public, yet. However, we do feel confident that we have the perpetrator in custody and that the city can sleep a little safer tonight."

"There is mention that Barry Finley might be a Satanist. Can you give us any information on that?" asked the reporter.

"I cannot comment on specifics," responded the officer, "everything will be available after the case has been made against the suspect and not before."

"Thank you, Officer Jacobs," the officer turned around and walked back to the house, "Well, you heard it here first. There was no denial that Barry Finley was a Satanist. I'm Mark Kelly from KISU news, back to you in the studio."

Kurt hit the back button and paused. He wanted to look further into it but noticed the time on the taskbar of the computer screen and knew he needed to start his homework before his dad came home or he'd be in a world of trouble. He reset the computer to the search engine home screen and took his books out of his backpack and got to work.

* * *

Detective Bailey sat in his sedan, watching the apartment complex across the street. He was hoping the kid would come to his car so he could ask questions but didn't want to make himself noticeable to others. He had his own secrets to keep and being out in the east part of the county wasn't part of his jurisdiction. He saw the other two kids stroll by who were walking with his target the previous couple of days. He was trying to get a sense of the times that Kurt might be alone so he could confront him about his phone call. So far, he wasn't having any luck.

He looked down at his phone and saw it was 5:48 p.m. Jim Palmer, Kurt's dad, should be coming home any time now, so he'd better get going. He pulled out from his parking space and caught the eight-freeway heading back towards downtown. He'd have to try again another day. He grabbed the cigar stub from the ashtray and absently lit it. He'd been working on it for a couple of days--a hobby, he chuckled to himself, and enjoyed the taste while he drove. The rosary beads and a crucifix hanging from his rear-view mirror jostled and swayed with the bumps in the road.

Finally, his exit came into sight and he pulled off the freeway into Normal Heights, a trendy suburban community of San Diego, north of the world-famous San Diego Zoo. A few turns later, and he was parked in the driveway of his very small, yet very overpriced home. It was a two-bedroom fixer-upper that wasn't quite fixed, but it didn't stand out and that's how he liked to live his life. He rustled through his keys to open the front door and hit the switch to turn on the hall light. Portraits lined the hallway, and he kissed his fingertips and pressed them to the faces on a couple of the pictures as he passed. After tossing his keys in a bowl next to his easy chair, he turned on the police band radio, like he always did when he got home, for something to play in the background. He turned up the volume a bit, then walked into the kitchen to grab a beer.

It was going to be another lonely night. He looked down at the side table which had a portrait of his wife and son who passed away several years before. Even though it had been years, the feeling of his stomach sinking gripped him every time. He wasn't so much in despair as he was angry with himself for not getting to his family sooner. Knowing who he was, if he had just been able to just touch them while there was still a breath in their lungs, he could have helped them. He looked at his hands, which should have been scarred from the embers of the house fire where his family perished. But the firemen had pulled his unconscious body out of the living room, where he had fallen asleep watching TV. His wife and son were in their bedrooms, already dead from the smoke inhalation. It was believed to have been arson, but no one had ever been caught. Steve had healed miraculously whole, but inside he would always have that missing piece. His anchor and his rock were gone.

Sitting down in his favorite chair, he took a sip of the beer when he heard over the radio a police bulletin about a man fitting his description stalking a young boy in the eastern part of the county. He sprayed the beer out of his mouth and spattered his TV set. *Crap,* he thought, *that kid must have talked to his dad and called in a report on me. Wiping his mouth, he reasoned, guess that ends it for the subtle approach.*

He continued listening while the description of his car was mentioned over the wire. "At least they didn't get my license plate," he mumbled to himself, thanking God for avoiding that awkwardness. He didn't let anyone know he was surveilling someone in the eastern part of the county, so getting popped for something like this would be a long story with a background he couldn't bring up.

Standing up, he crossed the room and pulled aside a portrait revealing a safe in the wall. With sure fingers, he spun the dial to the code only he knew to open it. After pulling the handle and opening the thick door, the inside revealed an item wrapped in cloth. He gently removed it from the safe and placed it on the dining room table. He pulled back the cloth on each side to reveal a leather-bound book with cryptic writing on the cover, understandable to Steve only after years of study. He slowly brushed his hand over the book, relishing the feel of something made so long ago and still here today. This book had been in his family for countless generations, handed down from father to son. Steve was the last to carry this book, and there were no more heirs to carry it. Right now, this was his birthright.

He opened the book to the first section and perused the heavy parchment. There were seven circles with Enochian writing above and below each one. Steve had learned from a young age that this was Angel hand script. He knew the writing translated to the names of the seven Archangels. He turned the page and a copy of the first circle and Enochian phrasing was listed, along with several other Enochian writings, then Greek, Latin, several languages he didn't recognize, a few resembling English, and finally English words. His great-great-grandfather had written those words into the book, he was told by his own father before he passed away. Steve always felt a connection to his family when he was reading this book. He used to read them to his own son, many years ago. He stepped over to take another drink of beer and then walked back to the book--he never put anything near the book which could damage it.

He flipped through the other pages of the book. Some other pages had writing, but nothing near extensive as the first page. The last three pages were completely blank except for the circle and the Enochian writing around it, identifying the name of the item. He went through the other pages with writing, except for the first, and tried to memorize the details. He had read it a hundred times, but he was looking for something specific this time. After going through the second page, he pulled out his notebook from his pocket and jotted down a location and color. On the third page, he scanned until he found another location and color, and wrote it down. He repeated the same thing on the fourth. For the blank pages, he just wrote down the colors, green, yellow, and white, and put his notebook back in his pocket.

Based on the locations that were known of the other three, this was a new player in the game. He would have to talk to the kid now, but how? Not wanting to get caught for stalking, he also didn't want anything powerful to fall into the wrong hands. Heading east wasn't a good idea for a few days until things settled down. Knowing his car couldn't be used again, Steve had to come up with a different idea.

* * *

Kurt's forgotten dream was always the same:

...Gabriel struggled with what he knew he had to do. He couldn't leave the Tree here to be destroyed by the Great Flood, but he also knew there would be a painful transition performed this day in severing the Tree of Life from the Earth. He didn't like the task but would never disobey a command from the Creator. He motioned for the other Angels to spread out to the seven outstretched roots of the tree, going back several cubits. When the roots were a handbreadth in diameter, they stopped. Each of the Angels faced inwards towards the tree and kneeled. Placing their hands around the roots, they crushed the root to break the tree's anchors in the ground. Their hands glowed from the heat and pressure. Gabriel could almost feel the Tree crying out in pain. As the bark and root finally gave way, he closed his hand, mirroring the six others around him. The Tree was now separated from the Earth. He opened his hand and saw the crushed remnant of the wood. With the pressure and heat, it looked more like a rock than a piece of root. He dropped it and walked towards the trunk with the other angels...

CHAPTER FIVE

━━━━━●◆●━━━━━

"Everyone, settle down," said Mrs. Wilson, the principal of Magnolia Middle School, as she spoke over the microphone to the students gathered in the arena. Sixth through eighth graders were making their way through the tiers of concrete, waving to their friends, and creating a general murmur that slowly increased in volume until the principal had to address the group again, "Please, everyone, sit down. We'd like to get this assembly started."

The rest of the school was indoors, like an indoor mall—all of the classes inside one building, separated by partitions. Being in California, the opportunity presented itself to have an open auditorium. It was set up in tiers of concrete bleachers in a half-circle around a stage where the speaker was standing. On the other side of the wall was the lunch area, also set outside with colorful picnic-style benches that were unoccupied during the meeting.

A female officer from the local police department was standing to the side of the stage with a megaphone. She put it to her mouth and addressed the students, "Everyone, quiet!" A pin drop could have been heard.

"That's better. Now get to your seats so we can get started." There was a large banner on the Drama Center building wall behind them that advertised "Stranger Danger – Call 911" and had a cartoon picture of a dog in sunglasses, a fedora hat, and a trench coat with the collar pulled up around his neck.

"My name is Officer Doyle," she began, "and this week we're learning about strangers, stalkers, and cyber bullying. I know you're itching to get to lunch but give me this time to fill you in about this information that could very well save your life!"

Kurt sat next to his friends and heard Alan groan.

"Hey, pay attention. Someone was after me the other day," said Kurt.

"No way," said Terence, "are you the reason we are having this lame assembly?"

"I doubt it. They don't put these things together that quickly," shot back Kurt. After his dad had come home the other day, he had told him about the stranger, and his dad called the police to file a report. Kurt assured him it wasn't a big deal, but his dad wasn't going to take any chances. They asked for details about the stranger, the car, location, time of day, everything.

On the stage, a skit was being acted out with the mascot of the school playing the kid, and someone from the police station, dressed as the dog on the banner. The dog was acting like he was a grown-up, trying to give candy or money to the kid. There were taunts and laughs from the crowd. The officer had to press the siren button on her bullhorn more than once to control the commotion.

"Didn't we learn this in kindergarten? Why don't they send us jugglers and trampoline jumpers like they used to?" asked Alan, "I'd even stay awake for a half-decent magician." Kurt and Terence laughed.

Down on the stage, it was back to the microphone and a teacher reading a story about a seventh grader getting bullied online. It was heart-wrenching and angering like it always was.

"Dang, who would let someone treat them like this online? I'd just delete my account and call it a day," said Kurt.

Terence shook his head, "Not always that easy. What if every friend you had was on that app except you? You'd be a social outcast in the real world for not being online."

"That's true, but it's much easier for kids to say mean things behind a computer screen than to your face. If you're not online, they can't stack up against you," returned Kurt.

Alan smiled, "Slam, he's got you there, T."

Finally, Officer Doyle came to the microphone to talk.

"There has been a rise in child abductions and child trafficking over the past few years. It is important that you pay attention to your surroundings, pay attention to each other, pay attention to your little brothers and sisters. Know where quick exits are. Know your address and phone number. Don't take shortcuts," she continued with her well-rehearsed, but poignant message. Her pleading lingered in everyone's ears until there was just silence. After a few seconds, the lunch bell rang, and everyone stormed away to eat. The staff on stage had various expressions, hoping the kids would retain something of the message.

A few hours later, after school let out, Kurt and the others were walking home when Terence suggested they go across the pedestrian bridge over the eight-freeway. "I hear they might be taking it down soon. Might as well get our last looks on it." They walked down

Green Street, which was off Oak Glen Road, to the start of the stairwell of the pedestrian bridge. There were notices posted about the upcoming demolition of the bridge. Yellow caution tape had been tied around the entrances, but the locals had torn it down. They would continue to use the bridge until they couldn't—it had been around for decades.

After climbing to the top and coming midway, the boys stopped, sat down, and just enjoyed the wind passing by while the cars flew below. There was a sign marking the speed limit just in their frame of view, but they knew everyone was traveling much faster than that. Californians were great drivers on the highways, just don't add a drop of water or they become the worst. They had heard the highway was expanding here, and the bridge had to come down, but they also heard that hoodlums were throwing fruit off the bridge at night into oncoming traffic. The smell of the oleander bushes rustling in the opposing traffic wafted up to them.

From where they were sitting, they could see someone walking up the same pedestrian ramp they walked up earlier. It was a tall guy in jeans wearing a black leather jacket and a motorcycle helmet. The motorcycle helmet was also black, and the visor shaded so you couldn't see his face. Once he neared the top of the stairs, he started to take his helmet off. As soon as Kurt saw those blue eyes, his heart jumped a beat. He whispered to his friends, "That's the guy who was asking questions about me the other day." When he heard the stranger call him by name, that was all his nerves could take. All three of them started running for the opposite side of the bridge.

Kurt was the fastest runner, but didn't want to leave his friends behind, so he paced with them. He spared a look over his shoulder and saw the man chasing after them. They had a good lead, but there was nowhere to hide until they got down below. Kurt, panting hard, told the other guys to split up once they got to the bottom of the ramp. He got confirming looks and a half nod as an answer. At the bottom, Terence cut left, Alan turned right, and Kurt ran straight, his bright orange backpack bouncing with every step. He decided to lose the backpack, so he one-armed it and tossed it in some nearby bushes. The stranger was yelling his name and telling him to stop.

Ducking through an apartment complex, Kurt slowed down quickly around a corner and hid behind a dumpster. He crouched down in the dark corner, trying to make himself as small as possible. He could hear his name being called, and the voice was getting closer. He fumbled with his phone to call 911 and realized his battery was completely dead. He stuffed his phone back in his jacket and tried to be as quiet as he could. He could hear the boot scrapes across the gravel of the parking lot near where he was. The voice was calmer, "Kurt, I'm not going to hurt you. Come out."

Kurt didn't trust it. He closed his eyes, wishing more than anything he was safe in his room. He could hear the footsteps getting closer, just as a soft green glow shone through his eyelids. He opened his eyes to see what it was and realized he was sitting on the floor of his room! He stood up quickly trying to get his bearings and saw the slightest glint of green from the top of his shirt in the mirror above his dresser, before it went dark. He touched the stone beneath his shirt, not understanding what just happened. He pulled out the chain to look at it, and the stone looked like it always had—just a regular blackish orb, no sign of any green glow.

He fell back into sitting on his bed. Leaning over and plugging in his phone to the charger, he rebooted it and waited till he could dial out. His first call was to Alan, who didn't pick up. He tried Terence and got through, "Hey, where are you?" he asked.

Terence responded, panting, "Down by the post office. I don't think he followed me."

"No, he was after me. I heard him calling my name. You can come back to my place, it's safe now," he responded.

"What? How'd you get back home so quickly?"

"I'll tell you when you get here. You're not going to believe me," Kurt said. *I don't believe me*, he thought.

He tried to call Alan and got through this time. "Alan, yeah, I'm OK. He was chasing me. Hey, can you get my backpack? I tossed it in the bushes to the right of the front entrance of the Mollison Gardens Apartments... Yes, the ones that are painted a kind of dark yellow and brown. I tossed it in the corner, so you'll have to hunt a bit, but bring it back to my place when you can... Thanks!"

Kurt looked at himself in the mirror. His skin was tinged a bit pink from running, but the freckles were still prominent across his nose. He stuck his hand through his brown hair to slick it back a bit. He thought of himself as the plainest-looking guy he knew. He wondered why the stranger could be chasing him. And how did he know him by name? It was just too creepy. He would have to tell his dad about this. His dad was going to be worried big time. Walking into the kitchen and opening the refrigerator, he grabbed a soda and sat on the couch to wait for his friends.

* * *

Steve looked behind the dumpster. He could have sworn he just saw a flash of light, maybe from the screen of a smartphone. Thinking he finally caught up with his target and now missing out again, he let out some choice words. Scanning around the area again, and finally giving up, he started walking back to the pedestrian bridge.

After crossing, he got back on his motorcycle and rode down the street to a vantage point on Oak Glen Road. He wasn't going to make himself visible this time, just watch and wait. He checked his phone, and it was 4:32 p.m. He had parked between a car and a van, so he could put his weight against the van and still look down the road towards Second Street.

Not more than twenty minutes later, he saw two of the three

boys coming around the corner, one of them carrying an extra orange backpack. Kurt was nowhere to be seen. The kids walked without a rush across the street and into the apartment complex. Steve was mystified. He thought for sure he would be able to pick up Kurt's trail coming back to his home. He waited until the other kids were inside the courtyard area and then he got off his bike. He locked his helmet to the side of the motorcycle and jogged across the street. Going in the direction of Kurt's apartment, he walked confidently toward it so as not to draw any undue attention. Once inside the latched gated area opposite the community laundry with six washers and four dryers all humming, he stopped to decide what he was going to do next. He pulled his badge and had it ready, covering much of the field of view of the peephole. If the kid didn't pull back the curtains to look through the kitchen, all he would see is the shiny badge. He might be able to pull this off without any hitches. He raised his other hand to knock on the door.

* * *

Knock-knock-knock. Terence and Alan looked at each other, then looked at Kurt, eyes wide.

Alan whispered, "Do you think he followed us here?"

They were apprehensive, especially after the week of Stranger Danger enforcement heightening their already jagged nerves.

Knock-knock-knock. "I know you're in there," came the voice through the door.

Alan yelled back, "We're calling the police, mister!"

The voice from the other side of the door said, "I am the police. Open up."

Terence crept towards the front door and looked through the

peephole. He turned back and mouthed, "All I see is a badge."

The voice piped up again, "There were some youths seen cross-ing a bridge clearly marked off limits by the city and reported to have come to this address."

"Oh, crap," Alan said, "we're screwed! Someone must have rat-ted us out."

Since the officer was obviously coming to talk to them about their trespassing on the bridge, they relaxed a bit. Kurt even thought they could tell the officer about the guy chasing him. He walked to the door and said, "Just a sec." He looked through the peephole and saw just the badge and the outline of a wallet, but nothing more. Bringing his arm up, he started to unlock the deadbolt. Before he had the chance to finish opening the door, it slammed into his face and pushed him back. The officer was rushing into the room, badge in one hand and taking off his sunglasses with the other. As soon as Kurt saw those blue eyes, he screamed.

"Shut up!" Detective Bailey said. Kurt stopped. Steve pointed to the two other kids and said, "I really am a police officer. This is my badge, and I need to talk to Kurt. You and you, leave now." He pointed at each of the boys when he called them out.

"Terence Jackson, son of Eli and Vanessa Jackson, date of birth April First, lives in apartment eighteen," Steve rattled off. Terence's eyes grew wide with the information.

Shifting his attention to Alan, he said, "Alan Watson, son of Bobby and Edith Watson, born January twenty-ninth, lives in apart-ment twenty-four."

He gave Terence and Alan a business card as each of them left and told them if they wanted to make sure he was a police officer, they could call his captain. He shut the door and told Kurt to sit on the couch.

Steve pulled a chair from the dining room and set it opposite of Kurt, and sat down. With a deep breath, he said, "Finally, we get a chance to talk." Detective Bailey was quite intimidating, and Kurt felt very uncomfortable. The detective took off his jacket, showing the holster of his gun on his left side. It didn't look like he had a bullet-proof vest on, just a regular button-down blue shirt.

"Look," Steve started out, "I don't have a lot of time to talk. I don't really want to involve your dad in this or your friends." When Kurt's eyes widened, he tried again. "No, here," and he reached up to his collar, lifted an ornate chain, and showed him the centerpiece. When Kurt saw it, he instinctively grasped at the stone around his own neck. Steve cried, "Ah, hah! I knew you had one, too!"

Kurt pulled his out, which was kind of skimpy compared to the interlaced chain that held the one on the detective's neck, but the stones themselves looked identical. He started to relax a bit. He was starting to get a little giddy, thinking he was going to find out how to use his stone. He winced a bit where the door hit him in the eye and brought his hand to his face.

"Let me fix that for you," said Steve. Kurt sat rigid, but Steve leaned over gently. Halfway to him, his stone was glowing a faint red as he brought his hand to Kurt's damaged eye ridge. With a smooth wave over the skin, the pain instantly went away, and he could see clearly again. The detective sat back, and the glowing subsided.

"Wow!" Kurt jumped up and looked in the hall mirror. There weren't any marks or bruises. It was like it never happened and the pain was a memory. "How? But… Yeah. But, how?" He couldn't get the words together and Steve just smiled. He had seen that reaction a dozen times in his life. "Does mine do that?"

"I have no idea," Bailey responded, "Until you called me the other day about Barry Finley, I had no idea there were any other stones on this side of the U.S. How long has your family had it? Which angel is it tied to?" He pulled out his notepad and pen and was ready to take notes from Kurt.

"Wait a flippin' second," Kurt shot back, "I just found this thing a few weeks ago."

Steve's face dropped. "What? You found it? What's the lineage? What's the history?"

"You got me," he responded, "I found it with a bunch of other rocks when we were camping up north a few weeks ago. If I didn't shoot it from my slingshot..."

"You what?!?" Steve interrupted, "These aren't rocks for sling-shots!" He stood up and started walking back and forth, combing his hair with his hands, "Do you know how rare these are?"

"Well, the second time I shot it..." Kurt started.

Steve couldn't bear it; he was completely flabbergasted. "No, no, no, no, no, no, no, no..." He waved his hand back and forth, "Please stop. I can't take it anymore. Just stop." The detective looked physically deflated. He turned the chair around and sat in it back-wards, folding his arms over the top of the chair and burying his face in his arms.

From the muffled clump of detective hump came the weak voice crackling, "Do you know there are only seven of these in the entire *universe*?!? And you were thinking it was fine to use it in your sling-shot?!?!"

"I'm sorry?" Kurt asked sheepishly, "Did you say, 'tied to an angel?'"

Steve collected himself, sat up, and began, "Yes, angel. Each Stone is tied to an archangel, or has something to do with the arch-angel, we don't really understand in our limited way of looking at things. For example, mine is the Stone of Raphael, Archangel of

Healing. You can tell the nature of the Stone by the color it emits while it's being used. It has been handed down through my family for eighteen generations."

"Really? That's cool," said Kurt. "But why can I hold it and my friends can't?"

"They know about the stone?" he asked. Kurt nodded. Steve wiped his face with his hand, "Crud, the less people who know about the stones, the better. You have a genetic predisposition to be able to hold the stones, same as I do, but not many people have the ability. I'll tell you about it when I get a chance to show you the history my family has kept.

"Your dad is going to be home soon, so I've got to get going. I've been keeping tabs on your comings and goings in the hopes of talking to you alone. Here's my card and my cell phone number. You can text me or email me. Don't call unless it's an emergency."

"OK, like I'm being chased by a crazy stranger?"

"Exactly," Steve grimaced, which made his mustache cover his lips, and walked back out the door. Kurt closed it and locked it up. There was a quick knock, and he opened it again. Detective Bailey was there. He stuck his finger into Kurt's chest and said, "Don't mess around with the stone until we've had a chance to talk again. These things are powerful. And don't let anyone else know about it. There are people after these stones, and they could do some real damage with them. The fewer people who know, the better. Anyone who knows is in danger." Kurt didn't need to be told twice. He gave a quick salute to confer compliance and closed the door again. He felt awesome but couldn't tell anyone! He thought about his friends and their safety and wondered what he was going to do to keep them safe or at least to make sure they didn't talk about the stone to anyone else. And then he realized, he hadn't told ANYONE about his sudden teleport to his bedroom. The detective had interrupted that story with his loud knocking. Kurt wasn't sure if it was a good idea to let anyone know, or not.

* * *

Kurt's forgotten dream was always the same:

...The Tree was now separated from the Earth. Gabriel opened his hand and saw the crushed remnant of the wood. With the pressure and heat, it looked more like a rock than a piece of root. He dropped it and walked towards the trunk with the other angels.

In unison, the angels lifted the Tree into the sky. While they moved further away from the land, the rain continued to fall, gaining in intensity. The small rocks, made from the substance of the Tree of Life and infused with the pure energy of the Archangels, glowed dimly, not noticed by the powerful entities who created them. As The Flood waters rose, the stones were scattered to all parts of the Earth...........

CHAPTER SIX

K urt got ready for school the next morning. He was standing in the bathroom, combing his hair. His dad had already left for work, so he was alone and anxious to try out the Stone, even though the detective told him not to try the night before. He pulled the chain over his shirt, held the Stone and said, "Bedroom," aloud. Nothing happened. Then he remembered he was crouching down before, so he did that and tried again. Nothing. No glow, no movement, he was getting bummed. He tried closing his eyes, but he still couldn't get it to work. Frustrated, he gave up, put his necklace back inside his shirt, grabbed his backpack, and walked outside.

He walked to the front of the apartment complex and saw his pals walking up to him. Alan started off, "Kurt! Why didn't you answer any of my texts last night?"

Kurt pulled his phone out of his pocket. It was completely dead since he had forgotten to plug it back in after all the excitement of the night before.

"Sorry, man, I forgot to plug it in."

Alan was fit to burst with questions. Kurt related to him and Terence about what he knew so far of the Stones from the information given by Detective Bailey, but also informed them of the dangers.

"You guys have to keep this quiet."

Terence looked back, "You know us! We'd die before anyone could rip the information from our brains." He was a bit over the top, but Kurt knew he was being sincere. Alan concurred.

"OK, after school, I want to go back to where we were yesterday and try something." Kurt thought that maybe if he went to the same location and did the same thing, he could trigger whatever it was that made the Stone function. He was out of other ideas at this point.

"Sure, no sweat," said Alan, "but we better get going or we'll be late."

The trio just barely made it to school on time, spending most of the trip talking on the way. They had to run when they got to the edge of the school property and heard the bell ring. The three split up to their own homerooms like they always did. After homeroom, Kurt had P.E. first period, something he usually looked forward to, but today they were doing the Presidential Fitness testing.

After Kurt dressed for P.E., he lined up with the other kids in the class to listen to the teacher's instruction on what they had to do today. He was dreading most of it, but the rope climb was the killer. He never built up the upper body strength to pull more than a few hands over before having to let go. He tried using his legs, but never could get the dexterity to make it work and help his ascent. He felt foolish scrambling on the rope with his legs kicking. But everyone had to do it. His dad had told him to just focus on the rope and do his best.

Kurt started out OK, with somewhat good results. He overshot the pushups by a few, and sit-ups by a few more, so he was feeling a little more confident. Getting in line behind several other kids for the final rope task, the kid behind him pushed his shoulder and said, "Hey, Kurt, are you going to weenie out on the rope like last year?"

Kurt turned to see Bill Mackey, one of the bigger kids in the class. Bill knew as well as Kurt did that few of the other kids ever made it all the way to the top, so Kurt was thankful he was in front of Bill instead of behind... Mackey was one of the kids who could make it halfway up. Kurt didn't want to follow him.

Just as it was about Kurt's turn, the bell rang. The P.E. teacher said, "OK, those of you who finished will go back to regular class tomorrow. We'll finish up tomorrow with those who haven't done all their activities yet."

"Whew!" thought Kurt, "put that off for one more day at least!" He ran back to the locker room to get changed. Bill laughed and yelled out, "See you tomorrow, Palm-less," a tired joke Bill liked to make about Kurt's last name.

The next classes seemed to drag. Kurt was anxious to get back to the spot he found himself yesterday. Between one class, he passed Terence and Alan and they high-fived in passing.

Finally, the last bell rang, and the three met up together and headed out of the school. Kurt told Terence and Alan how he got out of doing the rope test till tomorrow.

"Mackey is still bugging you?" asked Alan. "We should team up and kick his butt."

"Yeah," added Terence, "but you two first. You hold him down, and I'll pound him in the face."

Both boys made mock bravado attempts being boxing champions at each other before laughing and reducing it to a slap-fight. Kurt just laughed, knowing all three of them would get their collective butts kicked if they tried. He politically cut in to stop the scrimmage when it looked to get a little too severe and Terence was going to get smacked around.

They walked their normal path going home—they weren't going to cut across the pedestrian bridge this time. They could walk down Second Street and get to the same location from the other side. But after they jaywalked Main Street and turned onto Oak Glen, Kurt saw a familiar sight—Detective Bailey, but this time he was leaning up against a truck, looking casual, almost pleasant.

As the trio approached, Detective Bailey's demeanor seemed to dampen. Once all three were standing in front of him, he pointed at Terence and Alan in turn, "You and you, go home."

"What? Again?!?" whined Alan. Steve scowled at him and he didn't say anything more. Kurt stood still as the other two kept walking, their heads tipped down dramatically, with glances looking back.

"Why are you like that towards them?" asked Kurt.

"I'm just setting boundaries. The less they know about this stuff, the safer they are. I hope you didn't tell them everything?" asked Steve.

"Of course not," lied Kurt. He was loyal to his friends first, but he still wasn't sure what the danger was all about.

"OK, get in." Steve opened the truck door and Kurt climbed inside. He knew this wasn't normal, but somehow with the detective having a Stone, it made him someone Kurt wanted to trust. "I took a half day at work so I could get the things I was talking about and meet you here."

"Where are we going?" asked Kurt, after a few minutes of driving.

"Just down the street here. I have a friend who runs a martial arts studio. There are no classes this afternoon and he said I could use the space."

"Cool, I've always wanted to take martial arts, but my dad said it's too expensive." Kurt was excited.

"What's expensive is not being able to defend yourself when you're in trouble," responded Steve, "My son was a red belt before… before…" he trailed off.

"Before what?" prompted Kurt.

"Never mind. We're here."

Steve parked the truck, "I decided to rent a vehicle for a while since the El Cajon PD might be looking for my personal vehicle."

"Oh, sorry about that," said Kurt, "Should I call them and cancel it? You're a police detective. Can't you straighten it out?"

"No, don't worry about it. If you called and cancelled now, you'd probably get in trouble for a false statement. I don't need anyone to know my movements. You never know who might be listening. Now carry this, carefully." He put a book covered in cloth in Kurt's arms and went back to grabbing a few other folders. "This is everything I have regarding the Stones. I've been of the mindset that everything happens for a purpose. That means I believe you found the Stone for a reason. I want to show you what they are and how important it is to protect them."

Steve and Kurt got out of the car and walked up to the martial arts building. After knocking on the glass door, a face came to the window. A man opened the door and let them in. Steve introduced him to Kurt, "This is Grandmaster Lu, a friend of mine for as many years as I can remember."

Mr. Lu bowed and then held out a hand to Kurt. He was an Asian man of modest height and build, probably in his late fifties or early sixties by the grey in his beard and slight wrinkles around his eyes. Completely bald, save the beard and mustache, loose orange and white robes adorned his body tied with a black belt with intricate writing on it. Kurt's interest was piqued by the writing.

After shaking his hand in return, Kurt asked, "Those markings, do they mean something?"

Steve filled in, "Grandmaster Lu is one of only a handful of monks who have studied from the five monks of the Shaolin Temple in China who spread the martial arts after the destruction of the original temple."

"I can speak for myself, Mr. Bailey, but, yes, he is correct," Lu's accent was thick but understandable, "It depends entirely on who you talk to. Some say those who handed down the forms from Shaolin wrote them in a book of boxing techniques. Others say it was only by word of mouth from master to student that it was passed down. It was nice to meet you, Kurt. I have some things I must attend to." Grandmaster Lu bowed again and left the waiting room.

"So, what do we do now?" asked Kurt.

"Follow me," responded Steve, carrying the folders and heading the opposite direction of Grandmaster Lu to a room with a table and several chairs. There were hand flags and foldable number charts, so Kurt guessed it was used for sparring of some kind.

"OK, let's start at the beginning," said Steve, "Way back in time, after Adam and Eve, if you follow the Judeo-Christian mythologies, when the world was starting to populate, the angels would come down sometimes and procreate with the humans." Steve stopped for a moment looking uncomfortable. "You know about procreation and stuff, right?"

"Oh yeah, I had Sex Ed last year," responded Kurt, "We're good."

"What happened next was that the Nephilim were born, half angel and half human. These are written in the Bible as giants," Steve showed him a page copied from the scriptures with highlighted text. He continued, "Humans didn't like what they didn't understand, so most of the Nephilim were killed off, eventually. Some had interbred into human society so that they resembled humans more than angels."

Kurt's face spun towards Steve with eyes wide. "So, what I think you're saying is that we are descendants of these Nephilim?" asked Kurt, a grin peeking at the edges of his mouth.

"Precisely. Only someone with angel DNA, if that's what you want to call it, can touch the Stones. To everyone else, it's just too powerful. It burns to the touch for most, to others it prevents them from being able to hold it."

"Yeah, it cut my friend's hand," offered Kurt, "He was bleeding and everything."

"Whatever it is, no one without the right genetics can handle them." He pulled out the largest book from the cloth and opened the leather bindings showing the intricate script in highlights of silver and gold.

"Wow! This is amazing!" said Kurt, appreciating the age and the smell of the old leather. The parchment pages were a kaleidoscope of colors and shapes to his eyes. He could only read some text at the very bottom of each of the pages.

"Here," said Steve, "is the listing of all seven by name of their respective Archangel that each Stone is tied to." Kurt could see seven black orbs across the two pages, each with their own colored aura and strange writing above and below. He looked up questioningly.

Steve could see he needed to explain more, "That's Enochian writing, the writing of the Angels. If we get time, I'll teach you how to read those letters. But let me read these for you," he said pointing to the first one, "Stone of Raphael, that's the one I have." He pointed to the next, "Stone of Michael, Stone of Chamuel, Stone of Jophiel," he continued, "Stone of Gabriel, Stone of Ariel, and Stone of Azrael. You'll notice the colors associated with each Archangel."

"Yeah, I see Raphael's is red, and I noticed your Stone was glowing red yesterday," Kurt observed.

"Depending on which direction you want to look at the mythology, either the Stones' abilities were used to define the type of Archangel, or the Archangel defined the type of Stone. No one knows how the Stones were made—they have just appeared over time in various locations around the world. Some are passed down through families like mine."

Kurt's mind was abuzz with images of Archangels flying over the Earth, handing out powerful Stones as prizes for great feats in the past.

"Do you think the angels know about these stones?" he asked.

Steve shrugged, "I have no idea. It's hard to imagine they wouldn't know anything about them since the power is so specialized, but you never know."

"Do you think the angels came before the Stones?" asked Kurt.

"Since we have the recorded evidence of the Stones regarding the Archangels, I've always thought the Stones were made after. There are seven Stones, since seven is the number of completion mentioned in the Bible."

"What do you mean, the number of completion?" asked Kurt.

"The number seven is used throughout the Bible referring to completed issues or events. If you follow the Judeo-Christian mythology, the Earth was created in six days and God rested on the seventh. If you look in the book of Revelation, there are seven churches," answered Steve.

"So, whose Stone is green?" asked Kurt.

Steve's eyes widened, "Green? Yours is green? But that's Gabriel. His Stone has never been found." Steve rifled through the pages and pointed, "See? There's nothing written about it. If you have Gabriel's

Stone, that one hasn't been used in recorded history to my knowledge."

Kurt's heart dropped into his stomach. He thought he was going to find out everything he needed to know. "You mean there's nothing?"

Detective Bailey looked at the page, "According to this Enochian script, the green Stone is bound with Gabriel, the Archangel, Messenger and Traveler. That's all it says, but we know from the Bible that Gabriel was the Archangel who moved the stone from the tomb of Jesus."

"I was hoping for an owner's manual," joked Kurt half-heartedly. He was really bummed there wasn't more information.

"Well, I'll tell you something," Steve started, "The Stones have more power than anything these texts say they do. These are only the writings over time based on the experiences of the people who have used the Stones, but when they fall into a demon's hands, the power is much different."

"I thought only angels or people with angel DNA could hold them?" queried Kurt.

"True, but according to lore, when the greatest of the angels, Lucifer, challenged God's supremacy, he was cast from Heaven along with a third of the angels who followed him. These fallen angels became demons."

"Have you ever seen a demon?" Kurt's eyes were wide.

"Well, yes. And so have you. What you experienced in Mr. Finley's appearance on the news was a demon. While you have ownership of the Stone, you're able to see beyond the surface when demons possess individuals. Be careful, they are all around and you might have to pretend you don't notice much of the time until you are better prepared. On rare occasions, some descendants can see the demon's faces without the Stone. Those occurrences never turn out well."

"What do you mean?" asked Kurt, a little scared at the prospect now.

Steve went on, "Until you figure out what your Stone can do, it's more a treasure for the demon than advantage to you. Demons, being fallen angels, can handle the Stones and use them for their twisted ends. They can't take it directly from you, it would damage them the same as someone trying to touch it without the right genetics. Once it's on you, it's a part of you. You would have to give it to them voluntarily, but they are effective manipulators. You'll have to learn to master your Stone, so it doesn't end up giving an advantage to the other side."

When Kurt tilted his head in curiosity, Steve continued, "The demons are always up to something. I can exorcise them with my Stone by healing the human host's body from the infection, but I haven't found a way to kill off a demon, yet. You'll have to figure out how your Stone is going to be used in the same battle."

"Wait a second. I didn't sign up for this," Kurt said, "Can't I pass the Stone along to someone else who has the angel DNA to do this? I didn't know I'd be fighting demons."

"Kurt," Steve began, "like I said before, I believe everything happens for a reason. I think you were intended to find that Stone. I would venture to guess that your dad is not the line that your angel ancestry comes down on because he most likely would have found it. I saw from your file that your mom passed away."

"Yes, when I was young," Kurt looked down, "I don't know much about it."

"I'm sorry to hear that," responded Steve, "but it's likely the reason you found the Stone. Because if your mom were here, she would have found it before you."

Kurt couldn't wrap his mind around all of this, but he gave the detective the benefit of the doubt for the time being. "Hey, so how do I use the Stone or figure it out?"

Steve closed the book, put his folders together and motioned for Kurt to sit on the ground, cross-legged. He sat opposite of him in mirrored position. "Part of the key to accessing the power of the Stone is to have your mind clear of everything else. Have you tried meditation before?"

When Kurt shook his head, he continued, "There are many forms of meditation, but this one is very specific. It has to do with focusing all your reality and attention to one point in your mind to make something happen. You must encompass nothing else but that, and you'll be able to access the Stone's ability. You can't be thinking of what you want for lunch, or what the girls in second period said about you last week."

Kurt chuckled, "Hey, I think I know what you mean. But when I think I'm not thinking of anything, I have a ton of things going through my head."

"Exactly. In order to make this work, you must be able to connect to that moment of focusing on nothing else other than the intent of what you want to accomplish. And, hopefully, you'll be able to figure out what skill or talent that is in relation to the Stone you have."

"I wasn't going to mention this before, but since you said something, I think it might be relevant," offered Kurt.

Detective Bailey motioned for him to continue.

"When you were chasing after us yesterday, I was hiding behind a dumpster. I was crouched down and scared and wanted to be home more than anything, and then suddenly, I was in my bedroom."

"What? That's awesome! It makes perfect sense. Gabriel is

known as the traveler. Your ability would be along those lines. Can you do it any time you want?"

"No, I haven't been able to repeat it since," Kurt admitted.

"Hmm… That's probably because you're not able to concentrate enough on what you need to do or where you need to go. Here, I brought this book for you to read," Steve handed him a book on meditation. "Read the first couple of chapters. I think it might help. Until you get a handle on things, **be careful**. You wouldn't want to materialize in a mountain or a concrete wall. And don't let anyone see you do anything. We don't want to bring attention to ourselves. If the demons have a target, they attack in force."

Kurt didn't want to think about that. "Well, you could get me out and heal me up again, right?" he joked.

"We'll see about that. We can try some things another day. I'll text you the next time we can meet here. Since it's not far from your house, maybe you can just walk here. Or maybe, if you get good at that transporting thing, you can zoom right over." Steve smiled. "Now get going so your dad doesn't think you've been kidnapped. And here, take a flyer for a free month of martial arts. Maybe your dad will let you do it."

Kurt wasn't going to hold his breath, but he took the flyer anyway, stuffing it and the book in his backpack and heading home.

CHAPTER SEVEN

I t was near midnight and the nightclub downtown in the San Diego Gaslamp Quarter was packed. It was Ladies' Night, which always drew a large crowd. The High-Top, a virtually exclusive location on one of the four-story buildings in the redesigned area, attracted the up and comers of the tech, business, and financial world. Alcohol was poured liberally, and tabs at the end of the night were in the four figures. The staff was trained to accommodate the higher tastes of their patrons, including looking the other way if something less than legal peeked out.

Levi Mendez, a regular at the club, tilted back his eighth shot and slammed the glass upside down next to the other seven on the table, opposite another patron, holding the same eighth glass about to drink. "Your turn, my friend," he began, "if you can." He leaned back with a warm smile broadening his thin mustache. He was in his mid-thirties, but there were eons of parties in his eyes. Levi had been living this lifestyle for quite some time and always needed to push himself to get any type of satisfaction. There were several hundred-dollar bills laying on the table, soaking up spilled tequila, the pot for the winner. Several onlookers were cheering, barely audible over the thumping music in the background.

The opponent picked up his shot, a look of bliss on his face, and lifted it to his mouth. He leaned back and downed it, slamming the glass sideways and knocking down a few glasses. Levi stared at him for a while, then put up three fingers. He dropped the ring finger, then the middle finger, and finally pointed at the other guy. Within seconds, the other guy leaned over the side of the table and vomited, his girlfriend rubbing his back. Levi gingerly picked up the money on the table, cleaned off the excess liquid with a bar towel, and folded it into his pocket. He received cheers and a few pats on his shoulder from other regulars before he stood up. "I'll be back in a few for round two," he smiled.

There was barely any sway in his step as he walked to the restrooms. He was just getting warmed up and he knew how to pick his marks. He always had an ability to feel out other people and quickly size them up, which helped in some of his business dealings. Reaching the restroom, he stopped to look in the mirror. A blue, button-up shirt with a black blazer and black pants, the color popped out and looked good against his well-tanned skin. His hair was jet black, and he smirked at the peaks of the three sixes he had tattooed on the side of his neck that had driven his parents crazy before they passed away. He was their only son, and when they passed on, he inherited the Mendez MicroTech Corporation, a small manufacturing company trying to compete in the market with larger ones. But he had an idea that might just be the ticket to the big leagues.

He smiled and walked over to a stall, closed and locked the door, and pulled out his personal stash of cocaine. This was a more potent batch, he was told by his dealer, than he was probably used to. All the better, he thought. He took a big scoop with the spoon and sniffed it up his nose. Pain shot through his sinuses and then numbness. His nose started bleeding. He jammed toilet paper twisted up in his nose and leaned back against the stall door. Feeling free and easy, like he was on top of the world, he closed his eyes.

He couldn't tell if he was imagining it, or if it was coming from somewhere around him, a vibration inside of his head that was starting to form words. Then he heard it. A small voice asked, "Do you want to feel that good forever?" He slowly nodded.

"Do you want more power than you've ever had?"

The voice curled and caressed inside his brain, asking, "Would you give up your soul to have all the power in the world at your command?" He thought he must be dreaming. This was some strong stuff for sure. *I don't believe in souls*, he thought, *souls are for weak-minded people who can't function in reality.*

His eyes were closed, so he didn't see them coming, but a twisted insect cloud had been slowly billowing into the stall next to him from the vent above. The music in the club drowned out any noise the creatures could be making. Levi was leaning back with an open grin on his face when the swarm started to file down his throat. When the last of the insects had completed the run, Levi stood up, suddenly sobered, and removed the tissues from his nose. His hands steadied and his muscles relaxed as a sensation nothing really like coke overtook him. The Levi that he was fell fast away as the new demon mentality took over, reading his thoughts and history. A memory reminded him of the switchblade in his left pocket, more for show than use. Levi opened the stall, red eyes reflected back to him in the mirrors as he walked to the restroom door and locked it. There were still three other men in the room. It was time for a little fun. He grinned as the bolt slid in place.

* * *

The six a.m. alarm went off and Kurt silenced it with the switch. He wasn't fully feeling himself today as he had spent the better part of the night reading the book Detective Bailey had brought him. The first chapter just talked about why meditation was beneficial for everyone, but chapter two had some interesting practices to do. He had tried a couple of them before they put him to sleep. One was staring at a candle flame, identifying the parts, and focusing on the nothingness between the wick and color. The other practice had him sitting with his eyes closed and trying to think of emptiness. If a thought would come into his head, he wasn't supposed to go down that road, but encapsulate it in a bubble, and just let that bubble float away. He had a harder time with this method and fell asleep in the middle of attempting it.

He got ready for school as usual, but he wasn't looking forward to running into Bill Mackey again. Why some kids just liked to pick on others, Kurt couldn't understand. He wished someone would treat Bill Mackey like he treated others to give him a taste of his own medicine. With his backpack together, he passed the kitchen table and noticed his dad had left him a note and a dollar. The note read: "Treat yourself to a snack at lunch when you beat your climb last year. Stay focused. Love, Dad." He grabbed a banana and cereal bar, and headed out of the house to walk to school.

Like any other day, he met up with Terence and Alan, and before they had a chance to complain, Kurt put his hands up and said, "Wait till we're out of earshot of everyone."

They walked down the street quite a bit in silence until Kurt finally said, "OK. I'm sorry for how the detective treated you guys last night, but he's really trying to save you from getting hurt."

"How am I going to get hurt?" asked Terence.

"That's the problem," said Kurt, "If I don't tell you, then you have a better chance of not getting hurt."

"Well, that sounds like crap in a basket," said Alan, being as forthright as always. "How are we supposed to know if we're able to get hurt if we don't know what can hurt us to begin with?"

"Yes," responded Kurt, "you nailed it right on the head. Thank you. Discussion over."

"Wait!!" yelled Terence and Alan in unison. Alan continued, "That isn't fair."

"Life isn't fair," responded Kurt, a little too loudly. "How do you think I feel that I can't tell you things because it might get you hurt? We've known each other for a long time. Can you please, just this once, take it at face value that I'll tell you everything you need to know if you need to know it?"

"OK," said Alan, and Terence nodded. "If it's for our safety, we're going to have to trust you're doing the right thing. But don't ever forget that we're your friends, and we were your friends first."

"Yeah," added Terence.

"I get it, and thanks," responded Kurt. "I know who my friends are." But Kurt still felt like this was going to put a wedge in their loyalty.

They walked in silence the rest of the way to school.

The first period bell rang, and Kurt was changing into his P.E. clothes when he saw Bill Mackey already dressed out and walking ahead of him. "C'mon Palm-less, let's see what you can do." Kurt's blood began to boil. He finished dressing out and walked to the gymnasium to get in line with the few kids left to climb the rope. All the other kids were back in the courts playing street hockey, a game Kurt really loved. He couldn't wait to get over there.

"Alright, line up. Same thing as yesterday. You'll have two-and-a-half minutes to climb as high as you can. When you hear my whistle, you stop where you are, and we'll measure how far up you've gone. You need to make it at least to the yellow marker to qualify for the test," the coach pointed to the yellow tape circling the rope about ten feet up. Kurt didn't think he'd ever made it that far on the rope in the past. By circumstance, he ended up being last in line this time, right behind Mackey.

Three kids ahead of Kurt and Bill attempted their climbs, only one reaching the yellow tape and barely past it. The other two were far below—*at least I wouldn't be the only one*, thought Kurt.

Mackey walked up to the rope, shook his arms and paced back and forth on his legs, waiting for the coach to blow the whistle. Once he did, Bill jumped up on the rope, grabbing it only a couple of feet shy of the yellow mark and worked his way up the line. He grunted and groaned, used his feet and legs to his advantage, and continued upward. The coach was looking at his stopwatch, and then blew his whistle again. Mackey had made it seven or eight feet from the top, probably the best of all the kids so far. He slowly eased his way down and walked off the mats with a big smile on his reddened face. "Your turn, Palm-less."

Being last sucked. It wasn't just the normal kind of suck. It was the suck because everyone was waiting on you to go to the next event. *I am the one holding them back and I'm about to make a fool of myself*, thought Kurt. He felt all the eyes in the gym looking at him. Trying to center his thoughts, taking deep breaths, and focusing on the rope brought him back to where he needed to be. He walked up to the rope and took it into his hands, feeling the softness of the overused cotton strands. With his back to everyone else, he took in a breath. Closing his eyes and focusing on nothing but the rope and lifting himself to the top, he waited until he heard the whistle. When it sounded, he began smoothly, hand over hand, but it seemed easier than he recalled. Surprised by this, he peeked out of his eyelids, and noticed, below his cotton shirt, a faint glow of the Stone. As soon as he saw the green, his concentration was interrupted, and the Stone turned black again. His own weight suddenly got too hard to hold and he dropped to the ground. Bill Mackey's laughter was echoing from the walls.

"Can I start again?" asked Kurt.

The coach must have felt sorry for him, because he nodded, and reset his stopwatch for the two-and-a-half-minute climb.

"How many times are you going to dump yourself on the ground, Palm-Less?" chided a mirthful Mackey.

Kurt cleared his mind, focused as best as he could, putting everything else out. He only thought of lifting himself up the rope with ease and grace. When the whistle blew, he decidedly placed one hand above the other, and pulled. It felt invigorating and strange—like the weight was somehow reduced to something so small that it was easy to move around. He didn't bother using his legs, he just used his arms and climbed fist over fist, gradually at a moderate pace, then faster, until he reached the top of the line. He held the top of the crossbar the rope was attached to and looked down to see the coach checking his stopwatch. The coach bent his knees slightly and then blew his whistle. "Time!" he said, then he looked up and saw where Kurt was, hanging from the rafters. "Whoa! Someone's been practicing! How come the rest of you can't do that? Mackey, did you see that?"

Mackey was standing there, dumbfounded. He had nothing to say. He had just got schooled by the twerp he'd been dissing for years. Kurt swung down the rope, walked past Mackey saying, "That's how it's done." There were cheers and clapping from the kids in the gym, many who had been bullied by Mackey in the past. Kurt felt good about what he'd just accomplished, but he knew he also just made himself an enemy of Bill Mackey.

Kurt went through the rest of the day as usual, but from time to time he'd see other kids whisper or point at him. Between third and fourth period, Alan texted him that Mackey was on the hunt for him. By fifth period, the consensus was that Mackey was going to fight Kurt after school for making him look so bad during PE. Kurt didn't take that seriously. He'd never fought anyone before. Besides, with his newfound abilities, he thought he might be able to fend off a school bully.

After the bell rang for sixth period, Kurt gathered his things and left his final class. He walked outside where he usually met Terence and Alan on the south side of the school, but there were quite a few other kids gathered around. He met up with his buds and started to walk away when he heard Mackey call him out, "Hey Palmer! Where are you going? Are you chicken?"

Kurt stopped walking and turned around. "Why do you pick on everyone? Who do you think you are?" He walked up to Mackey and eyeballed him. He was a good three inches shorter than Bill. Even Mackey's frame looked more like an adult's compared to his own. He took a deep breath and tried to focus his thoughts together.

Whack! Mackey punched Kurt square in the face, knocking him to the ground. He didn't stop there. He climbed on top of Kurt and kept punching him in the face. Kurt could only see stars and feel pain. He couldn't focus on anything. He tasted blood in his mouth. The stone on the chain became visible to Mackey, and he tried to grab it, "Hey, this little sissy has a girly necklace on." As soon as he touched it, he reeled back and clasped his hand to his chest, blood showing through his white shirt. His wide eyes didn't understand, but, by the time he collected himself, a teacher had come and pulled him off. Kurt just lay on the ground, his nose bleeding, and one of his eyes starting to swell. Bill looked back at him and said, "That's how it's done!" and was escorted away by the teacher.

Another teacher came over to see how Kurt was doing. He was taken to the nurse's office and treated. Alan and Terence waited outside for him. After about fifteen minutes, he came out with cotton fillers in his nose, and a bandage on the side of his left eye. Kurt started walking off and the other guys fell in form.

"That Mackey is a punk," Terence said, trying to make his friend feel better.

"Save it," returned Kurt, "It's not going to make a difference." They walked for a while in silence. He wondered if his dad would let him take martial arts lessons after finding out he got beat up. There was the flyer for a month of free lessons. It might be worth a try. He was thinking of going to the dojo to watch, if nothing else, but the pain on his face let him know he was probably going to be staying home today.

After reaching their apartment complex, the guys said their goodbyes and split up to their own homes, having homework to do. Kurt, after getting in his door and dropping his backpack on the ground, slumped into the couch. He laid back and pulled out his phone. He sent a text to Detective Bailey, "Learned a new trick but didn't help when I needed it."

It wasn't long before he got a text back from Steve: "Talk later.

Busy. New case downtown." Not feeling all that great and not looking forward to talking to his dad later, Kurt closed his eyes and took a nap.

Chapter Eight

⎯⎯⎯ ● ◆ ● ⎯⎯⎯

There were a range of expressions on the faces throughout the room—from stoic, to frustrated, to concerned. Detective Bailey had picked up the job earlier that morning but had to wait for the Crime Scene Unit to finish all their testing and swabbing before he could enter. The officers had been collecting details from the patrons the whole morning and into the afternoon, letting them go after extensive questioning, searches, and warnings not to go too far. Steve walked past the bars and dance floors which never looked all that great in daylight without the neon lights sprucing them up, to the men's restroom where the incident had taken place.

It was a horrible scene. There were streaks of blood everywhere. Whoever did this was a sick, sadistic beast, thought Steve. The bodies were lined up in succession, carefully placed in order in the center of the room, meant to be found. When Steve reached the victims, one of the CSU agents lifted the shirts on the dead bodies. On each of the dead bodies was written a smattering of symbols that only

Steve recognized. It was Enochian, the angel alphabet, for "I know you." The lettering wasn't savage—it was meticulous, which made the hair on the back of Steve's neck raise. It was written with some type of phosphorescent ink to make sure it would show up no matter the lighting.

The CSU agent shrugged, "Any idea what that means, Detective?"

"No," Steve lied, "Not sure what that means." In his head, Steve knew exactly what happened. The demon he had exorcised not long ago had found a new body and was continuing its malicious attacks. There was no way to explain this to the scientific-minded CSU agent looking up at him, so he had to pretend not to understand the link. But, why would the demon be setting its sights on him in particular? That part of the message he was unable to grasp.

Unless the demon was trying to get his hands on his Stone. But the demon must've already known he couldn't just take the Stone away physically. There was something much deeper going on, and he intended to find out. He walked past the bodies and saw the window was open.

"But that's four stories. No one could jump that far down. He couldn't have gone that way," the CSU agent said. Steve walked over and pointed at the scuff marks on the sill. There was a blood-streaked handprint just outside of the window frame, not noticeable unless seen from the outside. Steve looked down and saw a glint of metal. He knew that would be the murder weapon, left behind because the murderer didn't care, and was finished with his work. He had done the same thing at the Connor's residence.

Turning back around and facing the agent, Steve said, "No, he most likely scaled the ledge and went through another window to try to prolong anyone being able to get inside. See if there are any closed-circuit cameras aimed at this window or the other rooms on this floor. We need to get a description of this perp as soon as we can." He pulled out his phone and texted Kurt, "Busy for a few days. Contact Mr. Lu. He will get you started."

Steve knew this was going to be a grueling process of elimination. He'd have to read reports taken of each visitor to cross reference completely who was present at the scene, and then weed out everyone who was left behind to get a short list of who might have been taken over by the demon. Again, that was assuming the demon wasn't already occupying someone and came in through the window prior to all this starting. This was not looking to be an easy prospect, but it came with the job. Rudy, his law enforcement partner, came by with a cup of coffee and Steve filled him in with his assessment.

Rudy was more practical in his approach to policing.

"Hey, this gobbly-gook written on the bodies. Is that some kind of Satanic writing, you think?"

Steve smirked and nodded.

* * *

Mr. Palmer came home to see Kurt at the table doing his homework. At first, nothing seemed amiss, but then he noticed the bandage on the side of his face. "What's this? Have you been fighting?" He almost said it in disbelief. He'd never thought of Kurt as being a bully.

"Dad, it's OK," Kurt said back. He explained what happened with the rope climb.

"You made it to the top?" his dad interjected.

Kurt affirmed and continued, trying to downplay his comment

made to Bill Mackey, but embellishing the part about Mackey taking his frustrations out on him.

"Wait a second, son," Mr. Palmer started, "from what I can gather, you did better than this Mackey kid on the rope and instead of stopping there, you poked the bull by saying something to him?"

"Yes, Dad."

"OK. That doesn't excuse what he did to you, but I'm sure you learned it's not good to rub people's nose in something. What did the nurse say?"

"She said nothing is broken. I'll probably have a black eye in a day or two," mumbled Kurt. He thought to himself, *not if I run into Detective Bailey during that time. He could fix me up in a snap.* He pulled the flyer from his backpack, "Hey, Dad, on that note, do you think it's a good time for me to start martial arts?"

"Look, Kurt, we've talked about this before. I wish I could, but it's just too expensive. When I was a kid, they were cheap, but now they aren't and require additional costs with belts and sparring gear. I just don't have the extra money right now," his dad responded.

"But, Dad, there's a whole month for free!" Kurt showed him the flyer.

"That's all fine and good, but how are you going to feel when you can't continue after that month?"

"It's better than nothing," he parlayed.

His dad put his hands up. "OK, OK…try it out for a month. Maybe I'll get a raise, or something will come up to keep you in there, but if not, you'll stop with no complaints, agreed?"

"Deal!" Kurt stuck his hand out. His dad took it and they both smiled. At least something good happened at the end of the day. *If this new ability isn't going to help me when I need it,* Kurt thought, *maybe I'd be able to learn some martial arts to avoid problems in the future.*

The next morning Kurt was practically jumping out of his house and down the sidewalk with excitement till he ran into Alan and Terence. "Hey, guys, look!" He brandished the flyer with his dad's signature on the safety waiver line. "I get one month of lessons for free. I've always wanted to learn karate or kung fu like Jackie Chan or Jet Li!"

"Cool," said Alan, clearly not as impressed as Kurt.

"I'm going right after school. Do you guys want to come with me? Maybe ask your parents if you can join, also?" Kurt suggested.

Terence spoke, "I know my mom will say no. I've already tried before. I'll let her know that you're going, but I doubt that's going to change her mind."

Alan shrugged, "My family's broke. Doubtful."

They were just across Main Street when they saw the video game truck unloading the new games to Kaden's Market. Strapped to a dolly ready to be wheeled in was the latest in a series of games: Eternal Kombat 5. Terence tapped Kurt on the shoulder, "Uh, I know where I'm going to be after school. Have fun with your push-ups."

"Yeah, I'm with you," Alan added, "Wouldn't you rather play video games, Kurt?"

"Nah… I'm going to try this out and see."

They continued to the school where they found out Bill Mackey had been put on suspension for his fighting. There were enough witnesses to collaborate that Kurt hadn't instigated, and Mackey would suffer the consequences for a week. But, then again, suspension from school for a week—how was that really a punishment? Hopefully Kurt wouldn't be his punching bag once he returned.

After school, the guys split up at Kaden's, Terence and Alan going to play the new video game, and Kurt heading to the dojo. He stopped by his house to get changed into sweatpants and a T-shirt, grabbed the flyer, and walked the rest of the way. By going this way, he passed under the eight-highway and got to see all the graffiti sprayed on the bridge over the years. Near the top in blocked black letters was written "READ 1 PETER 4:7." He mentally made a note to look it up since that was the newest scrawl. Last week it was something in Ecclesiastes. It was always cool to find out what was picked. He imagined maybe it was some secret code that people were using verses from the Bible to tell each other things.

A few short blocks down, he finally reached the Wushu Academy. The closed sign was up like before, so he tapped on the window hoping someone was there. Mr. Lu came to the door and opened it once he recognized Kurt. He bowed when he walked in the door. Kurt half stepped to bow in return, and then presented Mr. Lu with the flyer signed by his dad. Mr. Lu took it, set it on his desk, and motioned for Kurt to follow him.

They moved through the dojo, passing through the sparring room like the last time he was there. There was a young woman practicing alone on different movements. She was exceptionally graceful. Her uniform was completely white, which contrasted with her naturally dark skin, a worn black belt with several stripes finished her ensemble. When she moved in motion to see the both, Kurt thought he saw a wink before he was ushered into a smaller room.

Kurt whispered excitedly, "Who is that?"

"That is Bonnie," Mr. Lu returned with a knowing look. "She is in high school and teaches some of the younger students with me. Now, Mr. Bailey has explained the situation and has made available my services for you after school. I will teach you in the forms of focus and meditation, and if we have time, a bit of the martial arts, as I taught him when he was your age."

"But I have a month's free lessons from the flyer. My dad signed off on it and everything," pleaded Kurt.

Mr. Lu looked at him with the seriousness of decades and said, "I have the requirements I was given to make sure you would be suitably prepared to harness your destiny, Mr. Palmer. I have helped the Bailey family for two generations, and I was instructed to assist you in reaching your full potential with your special abilities. The lessons require no payment other than your dedication. Everything else has been arranged."

Kurt was stunned. He was starting to feel the seriousness of the situation, but he didn't know all the variables. He was both honored to be able to take lessons, yet at the same time didn't think he really had a choice in the matter. These conflicts were evident in his facial expressions because Mr. Lu stopped speaking, took a deep breath, and gestured for Kurt to sit on the ground across from him. Once seated on their feet with their knees in front of them, Mr. Lu began to speak softly, as though this were only for Kurt to hear.

"Throughout the times of man, set aside from the common history books, has been the unnatural warfare between good and evil. Many cultures view it in different ways, but the essence is the same. There is always the positive versus the negative. There are some of these that don't make it to the pages of your textbooks simply because there were no witnesses, or later scientists would rather dismiss the existence of such matters."

His voice deepened further, "I have seen the powers of Mr. Bailey's Stone. There is no doubt that these powers exist in the world. He tells me you have one like it. I do not have the prerequisites for handling such objects, but I have helped the family reach a deeper understanding of the item each held so he could shape it to better use in turn. Your priority here, Mr. Palmer, will be to learn how to use your Stone to your fullest potential, hopefully to assist in the balance of good. In my culture, we have other symbols to represent light and darkness, but we understand demons in this world, and continue to fight to rid this plane of them."

Kurt tried to take all of it in, but he wasn't sure he would be up to the task. Mr. Lu could see this was a lot for the shoulders of a thirteen-year-old boy.

Kurt felt his Stone under his shirt and lifted a hand to touch it. This was a lot, he knew, but he would try to do his part. "I will do my best, Mr. Lu," he said bowing deeply.

"I have been studying your Bible scriptures in reference to this Archangel Gabriel," Master Lu began. "There is not a lot of discussion of his actions, but I have the references from the Bailey manuscript. Tell me about what you have done with the Stone so far."

"Well, when I was hiding behind a dumpster and thinking I was going to get caught by someone who was after me, I closed my eyes and, then all of a sudden, I was home in my bedroom," Kurt responded.

Mr. Lu paused for a moment, curling his hand several times around his goatee while he thought before he finally spoke. "Archangel Gabriel is the Messenger or Traveler, so that must be one of the abilities. We will need to figure out what triggers the Stone to allow this to happen. Were there any other incidents which were enhanced by the Stone?"

Kurt told him about the outcome of the rope climb when using the Stone, which led him to want to learn martial arts.

"Wushu is for defense. I'm glad you have the mindset of protecting yourself rather than revenge. I assure you, once you have mastered your abilities, you will not have a need for martial arts. But, because mastering your body helps with the process of mastering your mind, you will be trained in some forms of Wushu." This garnered a grin from Kurt.

"I believe the second talent you mentioned might be easier to access. When I read the scriptures, Gabriel was the one who moved the great stone away from the tomb of Jesus. I would think this takes a great amount of strength. Once you can focus your mind in action, you'll have access to that strength you found before. The difficulty will be to maintain focus during distraction."

Kurt started shifting because his legs were falling asleep. When Mr. Lu saw this, he motioned for him to come to the only table in the room and sit down. He pulled a candle from the corner of the table and placed it in front of Kurt and lit it. "From the lessons Mr. Bailey gave you, study the flame. Study the parts of the flame. Separate the parts and focus on the nothingness within the sections. Do this for five or ten minutes each day to prepare your mind. Please come here after school on Mondays, Wednesdays, and Fridays when you don't have other commitments.

"I'll be right back."

Mr. Lu left the room for a few moments and came back in with a folded set of white clothing in his hands, and a white belt. He passed them to Kurt and said, "You have a different path to follow than the others who I teach in this dojo, but you will be tested along the way, nonetheless."

Kurt looked up from the flame and thanked Mr. Lu for the uniform before returning to consciously trying to empty his mind. He tried to move all the thoughts away, but his attention was drifting rapidly. He found himself getting sleepy instead of focused.

Mr. Lu noticed the lack of attention span and used his thumb and forefinger to extinguish the flame. "You can try this exercise at home. When you do, feel the energy in your body in connection with the Stone. While your mind is empty, try to notice something you didn't feel before you had the Stone and work with that. It's like training a muscle that you don't know where it is under your skin. If you don't know how to wiggle your ears, it's difficult to understand how others do it. You are searching for that connection to strengthen and have it become natural to you."

Kurt nodded. It was time for him to start heading home and the dojo to open for regular business. "I will try that every day, promise." Then he asked sheepishly, "What days does Bonnie teach again?"

Mr. Lu chuckled and said, "Don't you worry about that for now. You'll see her around."

Kurt left with the biggest grin on his face.

CHAPTER NINE

A couple of days later, it was Friday and time for Kurt to return to the dojo. He had been practicing the meditation instructions Mr. Lu and Detective Bailey had given him as often as he could in the hopes that it would make an impact on the mastering of his Stone. In the few days he had been doing these exercises, he felt much clearer in thought, more focused in his homework, and more deliberate when he spoke rather than impulsive.

Nearing the front door, Mr. Lu saw him through the glass and opened it up ushering him inside and locking it behind them. They moved to the previous room where they had talked before, but now there was a workout bench with an empty press bar and several cylindrical weight plates on either side on the floor. The bar was held aloft by brackets so it could be lifted in the bench-pressing position. However, there was a smaller, sturdy set of brackets lower, about the shoulders when lying down on the workout board. This smaller set appeared to be an emergency catch to avoid injuries in the event someone couldn't push the weight back to the top.

Mr. Lu motioned Kurt to sit on the workout board. He said, "Let's begin by assessing your normal workload. Afterwards, we will see if you can access the Stone to add additional strength to the process."

Kurt nodded and took off his chain with the Stone and set it on the ground near him. After leaning back on the workout board, he placed his hands equidistant apart, breathed, and pushed. The bar itself was only forty-five pounds, but for an undeveloped thirteen-year-old, that was quite a bit. He was able to lift it several times, but by no means without effort. By the last few, his legs were kicking out every so often to try to augment the energy in his arms. He finally let it rest on the high bracket.

"Now with the Stone." Kurt picked up the chain and put it back around his neck.

Mr. Lu spoke in a continuous, slow manner, "Keep yourself focused on pushing the weight. Try to feel a connection somewhere inside of you to the Stone and harness that energy. Try to sense something you haven't felt before and make that stronger."

He lifted the bar and put it on the lower brackets at Kurt's shoulders, then added two of the large plates to each side of the bar. "When you have your mind cleared, push the bar into the air."

Kurt was a little nervous, but since the bracket protected him from being crushed by the weight, he could take his time getting focused. He closed his eyes and tried to picture the room in his head. He omitted everything about the room except for his hands on the bar he was about to lift. Placing his hands on the bar, feeling the cold touch of the metal distracted him slightly, but he put that in a bubble and let it go. He refocused on the process of pushing the bar. He took a breath in, and slowly pushed.

To his delight, the bar moved somewhat easily. The connection between his will and the Stone was weak to begin with, but he focused on the bonding to accomplish what he needed. He lifted the weights five times in succession, each time getting faster as he learned how to tap into the strength of the Stone. He could feel it like an exoskeleton assisting him in moving the weight. Finally, he set the bar into the lower brackets and sat up and smiled, "That was awesome! Did you see that?"

Mr. Lu was smiling and already bending over to put more weights on. "Yes, that was an excellent first run. Based on how fast you picked it up, I'm going to add a few more of these on here to see how well you can handle more than triple your own weight. The Stone was glowing green."

"Wow! Sure thing!" Kurt fired back, anxious to go at it again. He leaned back as Mr. Lu was adding the last of the weights to the other side of the bar. After some quick calculations, he summed up that he was about to try a lift of four hundred and five pounds. He took another breath and released it slowly. Closing his eyes again, he focused and pushed. There was a little more resistance this time, but not much. He was learning to pull from the Stone's energy and utilize it. He hefted the weight five times again, reset the rack, and sat up.

"How did that feel?" asked Mr. Lu.

"You were totally right! It's like the muscle for wiggling your ears. You don't know how to describe how to use it until you know how to use it. I know where the energy is coming from, so I can get more when I need it," responded Kurt.

"Well, I only have a few plates left. Let's see how much you can do."

Kurt got back down while Mr. Lu added the last of the plates. There were now five hundred and eighty-five pounds to lift. He went through the same routine, taking a deep breath, focusing, putting his hands on the bar, pushing, feeling the energy, and using it to lift the weight in successive repetitions. He could feel a difference from the last one, but he still couldn't feel the actual limit to what this energy could allow him to do.

"That's incredible!" shouted Steve, entering the room. Immediately, Kurt's concentration was broken, and the bar fell dangerously towards his neck. Thankfully, the secondary bracket picked up the weight without hurting Kurt in the process. The green glow died out instantly.

"And, that's what we need to work on," said Mr. Lu.

A red-faced Kurt scrambled up from below the weights to see the others in the room.

Mr. Lu continued, "Kurt is going to have to find a meditation of motion state where he will be active but maintain that connection with the Stone, so he doesn't lose out on the benefits the Stone offers."

"So, do I need to find a different muscle for traveling?" Kurt pondered.

"No," said Steve, "you use the same connection. You just change the intent of the energy. Kind of like taking out a plug and plugging it in somewhere else."

"In that case, I could zap home, and then zap back here," Kurt mused.

"That depends," said Mr. Lu, "I don't think it works like an address book or map. There are a couple of ways the traveling might work. It could be by locations you are familiar with, or it could be by a pattern or something you recognize as a target to 'zap'. You may find yourself able to travel to your own bedroom, but not back here again because you aren't familiar enough with it."

"It's worth a shot," said Kurt, "worst that could happen is that I'd have to walk back here."

Kurt concentrated on the look of his bedroom. He felt the energy that he had access to earlier and put the two together. Instantly, a green glow encircled his body and he vanished. He kept his eyes open this time, so he saw the green take over his field of vision for a microsecond and then he was standing in his bedroom, just as he envisioned it. "Whoa! That was awesome!" he said aloud to no one who could hear.

He saw his backpack he left earlier and strapped it on his back. "Time to head back."

Concentrating as best he could about the dojo, he tried to remember the position he was in prior to traveling to his room. Nothing happened. He couldn't remember the dojo like he did his own room. He texted Detective Bailey to let him know it wasn't working and asked him if he wanted him to walk back. Detective Bailey told him to stay home because he was going back to the office and they'd catch up next week.

Well, at least I know I can get back to my room, Kurt thought to himself.

* * *

"No, that one," Levi Mendez pointed to one of the stands holding the suggested logos for his tech company, "that's the one I want."

"You got it," answered the ad man moving between the signs and grabbing the one he pointed out, "But why that one, it seems pretty simple? It almost looks like three ones next to each other instead of an 'M'."

"Because that's the subtlety of it, my friend. We will be number one in distribution, number one in technology, and number one in price. Bring it together, and you have M for Mendez MicroTech! It's poetry for the eyes," said Levi.

"If you say so, sir," responded the ad guy.

"I want the new logo on everything. Company hats, shirts, paper, everything," said Levi. "We've got a new product we're launching soon, and I want our logo to be the one everyone thinks about."

The promo manager made a few notes and took the stands from the room. Levi sat back down at his desk and reviewed the plans on the new Radio-Frequency ID (RFID) chip his company was working on. This could be a game changer, having not only the ability to store information for medical reasons but also to transact for sales, entry for private access, etc. The blockchain identity code on each chip was the key to keeping it personalized for the end user, while being quick enough to interact with outside technology.

Mendez MicroTech was already responsible for the Producer line, a breakthrough in the market where people have blockchain ID codes, and download purchased media like movies and songs, without the production of the physical tape, disk, record, whatever. No longer was there a need to create all the plastic—everything was digital and stored through ownership codes. A movie could be traded with another friend and during that time, the movie would be digitally unavailable to the original owner to preserve rights. Movies and songs could be sold to one another as commodities through an all-electronic platform.

It was all as simple as the old method of owning a "key-code" for a software package. If you had access to that code, you had full access to that software. The Producer line just made it simpler for users to conglomerate their media into one key. Not everyone had to have it to make the system work, but it was catching on, and Mendez MicroTech continued to enjoy the funding to supply their next line of technology.

The prototype for his new RFID would be ready in the next week for testing, a few weeks of trial runs, and then mass production. He was going to take information and media to the next level. He just needed to market it properly so everyone would see the simplicity in having this chip. No more carrying around a wallet—all your accounts would be computed into your chip, along with your transport rental information, medical history, the information limits were endless. No more magnetic strips wearing out, or chips breaking from sitting on them, or even the plastic. He was saving so many from the horrors of the ever-growing blob of plastic in the oceans. That would be a great viewpoint to sell – he'd have to remember to bring that up at the next board meeting. Levi spun in his chair and looked out the window over the San Diego Bay—quite the spectacular view with the sun setting over to the southwest. But his mind was elsewhere, thinking of the connectivity of the new chip and the hardware required for the point of sale. His mind was always racing, but it wasn't entirely just his. He didn't quite recognize the reflection in the window staring back at him with red eyes.

CHAPTER TEN

A fter an uneventful weekend, it was back to school on Monday. Bill Mackey still had a couple of more days of suspension, so Kurt relaxed walking about the school. The black eye he had started to fade to purplish yuck, but he was happy because he knew after school, he would be going to the Wushu Academy for lessons. After the last bell rang, he eagerly double-timed it out of the class and through the gate, barely allowing his pals to keep in tow.

Reaching home, he tossed his backpack aside and dressed in his uniform for his lessons with Mr. Lu. He sent out a quick text to Detective Bailey to see if he was going to be there, but Detective Bailey texted back he wouldn't. Kurt locked up the house and walked to the dojo.

To his welcome surprise, Bonnie met him at the front door when he arrived. He was just a bit nervous since she was a grade ahead of him, but he tried to play it off cool. Mr. Lu showed up shortly and said, "Bonnie will take you through the beginning katas. They are the basic forms which will give you a better connection with your mind and your body while in motion." He stepped back from the doorway with an outstretched hand and bade them to enter. He told Bonnie, "Take him through the first five katas, and don't let him move along until he masters each." Bonnie nodded and walked after Kurt.

Bonnie stood at the front of the classroom next to the rack of weapons and the mirror at her back. She motioned for Kurt to stand opposite of her. She put her arms back with her fists inverted by her armpits, and squared off her stance, placing her feet shoulder length apart. "Get into this position. It's called box-stance or first position." Kurt did the best he could to mimic her body, but he didn't have the years of experience to fall into it as gracefully as she did. She stood upright and circled him to review his stance.

"You need to separate your feet a little more, but keep your lower legs vertical, like you're riding a horse. No, don't turn them out or in, straight. Yes, that's it. Now straighten your back, chin up. Make real fists, not closed hands." Kurt was starting to feel a little embarrassed at this point.

Bonnie stood in front of him again and showed an outstretched fist. "Do you see how all of my bones line up from my shoulder through my upper arm, to my forearm, wrist and these first two knuckles? That's how to properly form a fist—that's where the power comes from. If anything is out of sync, you lose the strength in the punch."

Kurt heard the words, but he was only taking half of the knowledge in. He hoped his goofy smile wasn't as evident on the outside as it felt on the inside.

"And paying attention is very important," Bonnie continued. Then she placed her foot between his, pivoted, replaced his weight, and threw him over her. She followed the tumble to land on top of

Kurt flat on his back, her braids breaking free of the band holding them and forming a tunnel with their faces inches apart.

A sudden teenage awkwardness moment happened until Kurt said, with the wind half-knocked out of him, "I promise. I'll pay attention." She got up and gave a hand to pull him up. Another braid tie pulled from her wrist and Bonnie had her hair back ready.

Kurt tried to look as cool as he could for just being flipped over by someone in less than a second, straightening his uniform and belt and hand combing his hair. "That was fast," he said, not knowing exactly what he was referring to and feeling like he was glowing various shades of red.

"You have to be ready for anything," Bonnie went on, "always on guard, aware of everything. Now resume the first position and we'll start with the front punch." She led him through the first five katas, making sure he had them down completely before moving to the next. "There are nine practice warm-ups that we have, but the first five are the ones Master Lu asked me to teach you. We'll keep practicing these until he tells us to stop."

Bonnie showed him the first warmup, going through it again more slowly so he could understand. Kurt tried to follow her first moves and then she went on to the next warmup.

Kurt was starting to admire her form. The fluidity of her motion came from years of practice. She was graceful in her attacking exercises. He felt clunky and out of place next to her, but he tried. She didn't care about how he was doing, or was so used to it that she made no comment. He kept trying his hardest to copy everything she was doing with the flow that she did, but his muscles didn't have the years of preparation. This, he knew, would take time.

Cars were starting to drive into the parking lot for the regular classes. Mr. Lu came into the room and asked, "Bonnie, I have Doug teaching the adults tonight. Could you teach the kids?" With a quick nod and a smile, Bonnie took off to another room.

Once she was gone, Mr. Lu began, "Kurt, the ability for you to transport to a location must be defined by your ability to memorize that spot or have some detail about that spot that is specific. After thinking this over, I would like to try an experiment, if I may?"

"Sure!" said Kurt, eager to try one of his abilities out, "but, should Detective Bailey be here just in case I end up in a wall or a mountain or something?"

"That's a good idea. I will contact him and set something up on your training schedule. Good evening, Mr. Palmer."

* * *

"Hey, Steve," called Rudy, "did you see who you sent me to do that questioning about in that slaughter case downtown when you were out? Levi Mendez! Yeah, that Levi Mendez." Rudy sat on the corner of Steve's desk while Steve was trying to get his computer to turn on and drink his now lukewarm coffee.

"And I'm supposed to be impressed, how?" Steve responded.

Rudy countered, "Levi Mendez is the owner of Mendez Micro-Tech. Capice? Ring a bell? My kid just bought one of these Producer boxes he made or whatever they are, and now everything in the house is," Rudy used air quotes at this point, "useless. It's crazy backwards compatible. If you stick a DVD or CD in it, it locks in your ownership of that form of media, and you can get rid of the DVD or CD from then on. Anytime you ever want to watch that movie, you just stick your USB stick in the smart TV, and the app downloads whichever movies or songs you have keycodes for. That guy is going to be loaded when this takes over the market."

"Lucky you," Steve sneered back, somewhat disappointed he didn't get to meet this tech wizard. "But what does this have to do with our investigation?"

"Absolutely nothing," Rudy bounced back, "but, I thought you'd like to know."

"Consider me informed," Steve said as he went back to his computer.

Tim Jenkins, another nearby detective piped in, "Hey, are you talking about that Producer tech? I have one on my keychain right here." He showed his USB plug-in device and went on saying, "I just put this puppy in any computer or smart TV, and it installs the Producer App and I can have access over the internet to all of the movies and songs I've ever purchased. It's genius! I don't have to have DVDs, CDs, or wait for some streaming channel to have the rights to something. And since the companies don't have to produce the DVDs anymore, the movies are cheaper!"

"Isn't there something satisfying about having a library of books or movies?" asked Steve.

"If you really want it, the Producer App will create the graphical selection interface as shelves with titles that you can pick from instead of just a list. That way you can get your old nostalgia taken care of at the same time with the little pictures," Tim returned.

"But you can't hold a graphical interface," shot back Steve.

"And, you don't have to dust a graphical interface," rebounded Tim just as fast with a wink.

Steve put his hands in the air at face level, "OK, I give. You win," with a smile.

"You need to keep up with the times, old man," joked Tim, "things are changing all the time. I heard Mendez MicroTech is working on something big around the corner."

"Jenkins," Steve returned, "I can't be more than ten years older than you, probably not even that."

"And that, my friend, is the damn shame of it all," Tim said with a grin, "You have to keep up with the tech or you get left behind."

The sergeant on duty turned around the corner, let out a loud whistle with his fingers which got everyone's attention in the room. "OK, everyone, listen up. The chief is on his way down here, so look busy." The detectives went back to their desks.

The chief didn't come down to the squad room that often. *It must be important,* thought Steve.

Chief Hammond showed up in full uniform and hat with a grip of folders clutched to his chest. His face was heated and pink as if he had just got done yelling, most likely with the mayor or the press or both. He placed the folders on the podium and looked out to the detectives. "Listen up! I'm getting my butt handed to me out there with the press and the city because of these last three murders down-town. There couldn't have been a worse three people to pick out, one richer than the next, to make my job that much harder. Tell me, do we have anything?"

There was complete silence in the room. None of the detectives wanted to face the intimidating temper of the chief.

"Well, anyone?" His face was getting redder. This was not going to be good. Someone had to say something.

Steve put his reservations aside, lowered his head a little, and raised a hand.

"You, OK, whaddya got?" asked the chief.

In what was not common for Steve, he spoke up in a somewhat sheepish voice, "I believe it may be related to the Finley case."

"Finley is in custody about to go to trial. How the heck could he have pulled off these murders. What are you talking about?" blurted the chief.

"I'm thinking Finley had an accomplice or an admirer to his method. When we scanned the scene downtown, there were a few similarities that I recalled from the Finley case."

"Such as?" It was hard to read the chief with his thick eyeglasses. It covered his expressions so Steve couldn't tell if he was being sincere or sarcastic.

"Well, for instance," Steve began, "the sheer brutality of both murders was of equal level. Also, the weapon of choice, a knife, as well as the disposing of said weapon—right at the point of exiting the building."

Rudy looked at Steve, impressed. He didn't catch those details. Then again, Rudy didn't have the inside scoop as to what was driving the murders to begin with.

"OK, Bailey, you have a point on this one. Everything goes through you. And I will be in touch, so keep me updated on what's going on with this case. The press is like a piranha out there because of the status of these poor gents," said the chief.

Bailey stoically nodded. Great, he thought, just what he didn't need. A chief-level microscope on him all the time. He'd have to figure out what was going on with this demon and he didn't have the luxury of time any longer. He also didn't want that demon running around the same city as Kurt until he was able to learn his abilities a bit better. He was starting to like that guy. Kurt reminded him a bit of his son.

"Good. Everyone at ease." And the chief stomped off down the hall, with the sergeant in step behind him.

The captain smiled at Bailey knowingly, "Lucky you! At least he's not on my butt."

Steve gave him a sarcastic "thanks a lot" look. "OK, Rudy, let's get going on this case. Give me the files of the ones you interviewed when I was away, and we'll start getting things pieced together."

"They're already in the strategy room. I was starting a timeline to get a better idea of who was where," Rudy answered back.

"Excellent idea. I was going to propose the same. Let's get to it."

Both detectives headed down the hallway for what was sure to be a very long night.

CHAPTER ELEVEN

A week had passed, and it was the day Bill Mackey was to come back to school. Kurt was feeling a little trepidation not knowing how the first contact would be. He didn't think it was going to be all candy and roses, but he was hoping to avoid another black eye as the one he had was almost gone. He was pondering this during homeroom when he heard his name and Mackey's over the intercom requesting them to come to the principal's office. Everyone turned to look at Kurt as he got up and slowly took his things with him to the door.

When Kurt arrived at Mrs. Wilson's office, Bill was already there, sitting in a chair opposite the principal. His head was tipped down a bit and he was biting at his bottom lip. When he saw Kurt enter, his head didn't move much, but his eyes rolled to the corners focusing on Kurt with an angry glare. Even his jaw moved out a bit. There was no hiding his feelings. Mrs. Wilson cleared her throat and said, "Boys, it's important that everyone gets along at school. This is a location of education and harmony." Mackey wasn't hearing any of it.

Mrs. Wilson went on for a few minutes about how students should behave themselves and how they should conduct their day-to-day activities. Finally, she said, "and I'd like you two to shake hands, so I know you won't be fighting any longer."

Bill smiled, "Yeah, I have no problem shaking hands," and put his hand out.

Kurt knew what Mackey was up to, but he wasn't going to allow him to intimidate. He calmed himself with his breathing techniques and took Bill's hand. Mackey was trying to look nonchalant while steadily squeezing Kurt's hand harder and harder. But Kurt was ready this time. He pulled on the energy of the Stone and applied the strength to Mackey's hand. At first, it was a stalemate, but then Bill's eyes started to widen a little and water. Kurt applied just a little more pressure and Mackey yelled out, "Uncle." Kurt let go and Mackey held his hand to his chest.

"There we go!" said Mrs. Wilson, "Now, get back to class. First period is about to begin."

Walking out the doorway, Kurt mumbled to Mackey, "I'm not one to mess with anymore. I can do a lot more than that. I wasn't even trying hard."

Bill could see that Kurt was being serious. He said back, "You're a freak, Palmer! You just stay away from me!" Kids in the hallway turned to look at the spectacle. Kurt just stood there while Mackey walked away. After a while, the kids filled the space between, but those words stuck in Kurt's head.

It was hot outside during the lunch period. The sun was beating down without a cloud in the sky to diffuse the intensity. The occasional yellowjacket or Africanized honeybee was darting around the trashcans where containers of fruit punch and apple juice were discarded. Mackey and a couple of his buddies were using pencils with the erasers pulled off and clamped shut to flick the stingers off the bees and watch how long the bee would stay alive without the lower half of its body.

Alan and Terence were saving a seat for Kurt who was in line to get his lunch. They saw Mackey coming and tried to blend into the surroundings, but Bill already had his eye on them. As he approached, Alan piped up, "Yeah, everyone heard what Kurt did to you this morning. You better watch out."

Terence added, "Yeah."

Mackey took Terence's hat by the bill and pulled it down over his face and pushed him back into the seat he was rising from. Then, he turned to Alan, "I'm not afraid of anyone in this school, least of all you, Watson," and grabbed him by the shirt collar front.

A small crowd had started to gather around the event. Mackey was pointing his finger in Alan's face when he felt a tap on his shoulder.

"I believe you are......" Kurt started, but Mackey immediately turned around and tried to throw a punch to Kurt's face. Kurt was prepared this time. He opened his hand and caught Bill's hand mid-flight and the punch stopped cold. Mackey's eyes shot wide open in confusion. Kurt was connected to the energy of the Stone and able to draw on its power and a small smile crossed his lips.

"Whaa..." was all Mackey could say before Kurt grabbed him by the belt and lifted him overhead and carried him over to the school fountain. He unceremoniously dropped Mackey with a splash into the water. Bill hit his arm on the concrete side of the fountain on the way down and when he gained his footing in the water, he clutched his arm and was crying out in pain. The lunch attendant ran over to assist Bill in getting out of the fountain.

When Kurt looked around, expecting to see hoorahs for his beating of the bully, instead he saw faces filled with shock and horror. Friends he had just minutes ago didn't recognize him. He started to walk towards the crowd of kids, and several of them backed up in terror—some kids ran off in fear. Most were just stunned at what they just witnessed.

Kurt turned and ran away, realizing he'd just turned into the bully he was trying to quash. And now he was responsible for breaking someone's arm on top of humiliating him in front of everyone. He ran to where he had left his backpack, swept it up, and kept running. When he was sure no one could see him on the other side of the gym, he transported himself to his bedroom, threw down his backpack, and climbed into his bed, tossing the pillow over his head and sobbed to himself.

A while later, his phone's text notification stirred him from a restless nap. The message was from Mr. Lu to have him come down to the dojo straight after school. He really wasn't feeling up to it, but he threw on his sweatpants and a T-shirt and headed out to the Academy.

When Kurt reached the location, Mr. Lu and Detective Bailey were already there. Mr. Lu noticed Kurt was looking crestfallen and asked what was going on. Kurt filled him in on the details of the day. Mr. Lu's face grew taught during the telling, and then softened when he said, "Kurt, the reason we train is to defend ourselves. Whether by fist, by foot, or by supernatural abilities, we must keep this in focus. You were not defending yourself when you threw Mackey into the fountain. The only creatures we attack are the demons, and that is to defend humanity from them. It may not be my place to admonish you for what you have done, but if you continue to misuse your abilities, you will no longer be welcome here."

Kurt's face dropped and he appeared as though he would break into tears again. "I promise I will be more careful." He bowed low to Mr. Lu while Detective Bailey watched on with a concerned look on his face.

Mr. Lu put his hand on Kurt's shoulder and said, "Let's focus on what I called you in for today." Kurt nodded in silence.

Kurt walked ahead and Mr. Lu said quietly to Steve, "Reminds me of a similar situation a long time ago. Do you happen to remember that?"

Steve smiled, "Yes, but I don't recall your letting me get off that easy."

Mr. Lu looked back at him, "He has a good heart and a strong sense of justice. These are good attributes to build upon. I would rather nourish the positive than strike out the negative, given the choice."

"Wait, you made me do push-ups and run miles, if I recall correctly," commented Steve.

"Yes, I'm still working on you," Mr. Lu laughed, patting Steve on the shoulder.

All three walked into one of the smaller rooms where everything had been cleared out except for a large patterned mat in the center of the room. The pattern was simple, but very distinct, having only two geometric shapes with Kurt's name written in black marker in the corners. Mr. Lu pointed at the mat and said, "I bought this at a rug shop nearby, along with other patterned mats of various sizes. I wanted to see if you could memorize the pattern and then be able to phase to that location from another area. Please study this pattern for a few minutes to get familiar with it."

Kurt sat down at the base of the mat and looked at the triangle and square on the mat, along with his name written in each corner exactly the same way. When he felt he had the pattern memorized quite clearly, he indicated he was ready. Mr. Lu led him to a different room and then came back to watch with Detective Bailey. After a few seconds, there was the slightest green glow above the rug just before Kurt popped into view.

"Holy cow, I'm never going to get used to that," said Steve.

Mr. Lu asked, "How hard was it to transport this time, Kurt?"

Kurt shrugged, "It was pretty easy. I had the pattern of the mat in my head, connected it with the energy and suddenly I was here. But, why would it work for my bedroom?"

Mr. Lu explained, "It appears your Stone needs a unique location in order to transfer. Had the mat not had your name in the corners, you could have turned up on any of a thousand similar mats made, but because I altered it to become unique, it was like a signature for you to follow. Your room is very familiar to you, and it is unique. What you will need to do is practice looking for things that make a location one-of-a-kind and memorize that. Then you'll have a ticket to that location in your head any time. I have various sized mats similarly marked because I wanted to see what the smallest configuration of a pattern is required for your transport."

"This is why I brought you to Master Lu," said Steve, "Only he could figure out these kinds of things. He helped me quite a bit when I was growing up with my Stone."

Kurt was grateful and ready to try the next test. Mr. Lu set up a series of mats from the first one being eight foot by ten foot down to the smallest about the size of a washcloth. Kurt was able to transport every time he could memorize the pattern. After that, he told Mr. Lu to hold the mat and stand back. He walked to the other room as before. In a few moments, the green glow appeared, and Kurt popped into existence again.

Kurt explained, "I think I'm getting the hang of this. Being in this room so much today, I could remember details to get myself back."

Steve and Mr. Lu were all smiles and patting Kurt on the back. Steve started, "That was awesome! Now you have a formidable defense against the demons. If all you-know-what breaks out, you can transfer to a safe location."

Kurt put his hand out to shake with Steve. Steve put his hand out. When they clasped, Kurt smiled and winked. Steve's eyes got wide when he realized what was about to happen. And then…

…poof. They were in Kurt's bedroom. With Steve's size, the room felt a little cramped, but Steve was more in shock than anything else. Kurt chuckled, "You should see the look on your face!"

When Steve was able to recover himself a bit, he began, "So, that's what it's like? That's pretty disorienting."

"Maybe not so much for me because I know where I'm going," said Kurt.

"There is that," admitted Steve, "This room looks as messy as my son's was."

"What happened to your son," asked Kurt, "if it's not too bad to ask?" Steve gestured and they sat down.

"I don't like talking about it, but who better to confide in than another carrier of a Stone?" he said brandishing a half-grin.

"Connie and I were high school sweethearts, and we married shortly after I graduated from the police academy. She continued through school to become an elementary teacher. After a few years we decided it was time to have kids. After Christopher was born, there were freezes on increases in income at the department. Shortly after were the teachers' union strikes. We didn't know what was going to happen, but we knew we couldn't afford another child, so we postponed until we had a more stable financial situation. Months turned into years, and we just settled into the idea of only having one child.

"Christopher was a great kid with the heart of a saint. I don't know how I lucked out, but he was kind and generous to a fault. Of course, I am probably a bit biased. However, I don't recall ever having to reprimand him more than raising my voice or giving him a stern look. He was going to inherit the Healing Stone after me. There wasn't a better person for that Stone than him. I imagine he could have cured the world of all of its wrongs. We would sit down and read the books and letters together so he could learn the different languages. He was picking up the Enochian so well.

"But some arsonist decided that my house was a tinderbox and lit it on fire. I was asleep in the living room having dozed off after watching the football game on Monday night. Connie and Christopher were in their rooms in the back of the house where the fire started. From what the paramedics told me, it's likely they never woke up from the smoke inhalation and lack of oxygen. My Stone was going to keep me alive regardless of the fire, just on the nature of it. The paramedics were surprised when I got up and raced back into the house to save my family. I burned my hands on the doorknobs, smelled my skin cooking, but I didn't care. I had to reach them, but it was already too late.

"What I brought out were lifeless reminders of a happier time. I was crushed inside. It was a pain that the Stone couldn't begin to heal." Steve had to stop for a moment because he was choking up a bit. His fist came to his lips while he tried to steady himself again. "That was almost two years ago, and no one has caught that arsonist, yet. I'm too close to the case so they won't let me work it. He was eleven … only eleven." Steve's head dropped down into his hands as he continued, "I spent a few months off the job in therapy. There's no way to truly heal from that kind of loss. If I didn't have my faith, I probably would have lost my mind."

"I'm so sorry," said Kurt. "He'd be my age now. My mom passed away when I was younger, but it's not the same because I still had my dad."

"I had these coins made that I carry around every day," Steve said, handing them to Kurt so he could look at them. "They are titanium, so they don't rust or tarnish."

Kurt held the coins reverently. Each was the size of a half-dollar. An impression of a child's face was etched on the side of one and a woman's face on the side of the other, along with their names and dates of life. On the reverse of each were a pair of angel wings, a small crucifix, and a Scripture reference—Matthew 19:14 on Christopher's coin and 1 John 4:7 on Connie's coin. Kurt felt overwhelmed as he handed the coins back to Steve.

Just then, they heard the front door open and Mr. Palmer announced he was home. They had been talking for a while and not paid attention to the time. Kurt started to wonder what to do. Steve quietly calmed him down and told him softly to focus, and whispered, "you got this." Kurt nodded and reached out his hand to Steve's shoulder. With a shimmer and inward rush of air, they were gone, just as the door to his room started to open.

Mr. Palmer stuck his head inside and looked around talking to himself, "I could have sworn I heard someone back here. Oh well, must be the neighbors—thin walls. I wonder where that kid is." He turned and closed the door, heading to the kitchen to get his phone.

CHAPTER TWELVE

"So, that's it?" asked one of the people gathered around the table for the conference. Levi Mendez held up an implant barely half an inch long. It was cylindrical on one side, but flat on the other, except for the company logo embossed on the surface.

"Why add your company logo if it's going under the skin, anyway?"

Levi leaned back in his chair. "That's a good question. In fact, when I talked to the engineers, they said they needed these lines here for the heat distribution and mounting of certain parts, so I just suggested they add the design since the lines were there already."

Levi paused to gauge the room and then smiled, "And now, ladies and gentlemen, I am going to be testing out the first, just off the line. We designed it to go in the right hand, between the thumb and forefinger." Levi put out his hand and a lab technician took a few timid steps closer with an injection device. He placed the tube's end in the area on Levi's hand, and pressed a button on the box the tube was attached to. There was a little air pressure 'pip' sound, then the process was done. Levi lifted his hand up to show those in the room. A barely noticeable cut that had already been sealed over was all there was to show for the injection

"What this fantastic device does is insert the implant with a cold cut, so cold you can barely feel it, placing the implant into the correct space, and then seals it with a liquid bandage substrate. A fourth grader could operate this machine, no harm intended, Mr. Garcia," said Levi with a bright grin on his face.

"We're not to the point of mass marketing the injectors, yet, but we'll get there. As of right now, the implants must be injected at the factory. So, enough for the gory parts, let's see the fun parts!"

Mr. Mendez walked over to the second table where he had some of what looked like his Producer line of equipment on the table. He turned suddenly when it appeared someone was trying to film him with his smartphone. "Security, get that phone! There is no videotaping of any kind here today. You can watch, draw, whatever else, but no video." Two bullish men took the guy in lockstep down the hall.

"Now, you were exclusively invited to this product launch, and I would appreciate it if you would maintain the rules. Everyone good? Great! I don't go out in public much, so consider yourselves very lucky to be invited to this groundbreaking event that will revolutionize commerce and information as we know it."

He went back behind the table with the different items and started pointing to them, "Remember this Producer model that you had to have a USB keycode to activate? And what if it was broken, or you lost it, or someone stole it? Now, here is the solution!"

Levi waved his hand over the next similar box and its electronics sprang to life. The display setting on the front said, "Welcome, Levi

Mendez. What would you like me to play from your selections?" A few of the people in the audience nodded their heads that they were impressed. Levi pointed out, "It's on mute, so you don't hear the various vocal settings, but they are all available and easily set. Now over here, we have a simulation of visiting a physician."

One of the lab technicians filling in as a doctor came over with a folder filled with papers about an inch thick. Levi began, "Now, imagine your doctor has to go through all of these papers to diagnose what you have or see if there's a contraindication of one of your prescriptions. It would be much simpler for him to do this."

The technician dropped the file on the table with a bang and took a device from his pocket and waved it over Mr. Mendez's right hand. On the monitor behind them, data was streaming so fast it was a blur. "All of my medical history, available in digital readiness, in mere seconds anywhere I go in the world. These implants have memory to expand the items needed in the medical file, or any other file you decide to carry with you."

A gentleman in the middle of the crowd raised his hand and asked, "What if I chopped off your hand? Could I use it to get money from a teller machine?" This generated quite a few laughs in the audience, but Levi was ready for the question.

"If you collected a few in a sack, that would give a new meaning to the phrase 'Handbag,' wouldn't it? But in all seriousness, as soon as the implant is placed in the host's biology, it maintains readings on that person's vital signs. If the readings indicate a death or near death, the implant automatically ceases to function in its primary role and becomes a beacon. If you were to cut off my hand, it would lead the police directly to you," Levi said with a smile.

"Another question over here," said a portly gentleman, "why is it that you chose the right hand only for this, and what if the person doesn't have a right hand?"

"Excellent questions! As to the first, I'm left-handed, and if something were to go horribly wrong, I didn't want it to go wrong on my dominant hand. So, I made all the point of sale and terminal coding for a right-handed implant to keep uniformity. It's about time us southpaws got one back on everyone else. As for the other issue, we have another similar implant that can go on your head just at the hairline so it's not noticeable. Bear in mind, also, that this technology can be integrated with existing technologies like mouse control and keyboards, which are generally favored to the right hand already.

"I think we have time for one more question," said Levi.

Several hands raised in unison to Levi's delight. His smile widened as he selected the person he thought would be the hardest to convince to participate, "Yes, you over there, please, what's your question?"

An older lady with grey hair pulled back in a bun and several coats of make-up to soothe her vanity asked, "What's the price point we are talking about? Is this something the common person can get over the counter?"

Levi was waiting for this question. "Ladies and gentlemen, I want to make this product free to anyone who wants it." Gasps were in the air. Levi quickly put a hand up, "Wait, wait, wait... Please pay attention. Everything is dependent on this implant being inside the hand. We have subscriptions tied into every service we have available for every product line out there. We can absorb the costs of these chips through the subscriptions, and mass market them to everyone. Once everyone has one of these in their hands, all the commerce in the world will be flowing through your bank accounts!"

That brightened up everyone's eyes. Levi was grinning ear to ear. He was going to single-handedly redevelop the way things were

traded, marketed, sold, and used in the next few years. All he needed was these fat cats' money to grow the business exponentially to
expand to every corner of the planet. And he hit them where it felt
the best, right in the wallet. The investors couldn't offer their money
fast enough to get a percentage deal of the subscription services
provided.

"Whoa, hold on now, everyone will get a turn," said Levi. He
turned to one of his underlings and a couple of his lawyers, and
whispered to them. After a moment he said, "I have some business
I must investigate, but my associates here will be taking your offers
on my behalf."

Levi left the room with a couple of his employees. After closing
the door and walking down the hall, one of the employees opened
with, "Mr. Mendez, the gentleman with the phone wasn't connected
to any outside carrier when he made the recording, and it didn't leave
the building. He was taping only and not broadcasting."

"Good," said Levi, "make sure the video is wiped completely
before returning the phone to the owner. I can't afford to have any
of this information leaked out to the public earlier than what we
have planned for marketing. Anything they say publicly can only be
assumed as 'hopeful thinking' without video proof."

*And, I can't have any rogue detective stopping me from fulfilling my destiny
by being able to see me. I will have that Stone one way or another,* he thought
to himself.

"When you're done with that, have the reports brought to my
office."

The men left and Levi proceeded to go to his office. He took off
his jacket and put it on the stand near the door. There was a shower
and kitchenette behind the door to the back of his office, for days
when he would work late. Lately, he had been staying at the office

around the clock and had been having his service people bring his laundered items to his office. There was so much to do to get ready for this launch, he had practically moved into his building. It also prevented him from having to go too often into public spaces where he might get viewed on camera or in passing by that detective. Eventually, he'd be powerful enough where it wouldn't make a difference, but that time wasn't now. He eased himself down at his desk and waited for the generous reports to come in.

* * *

"You know they have computers for that now," taunted Detective Tim Jenkins while passing by the strategy room's bulletin board.

"Yeah, yeah, we know, but this makes us feel better, OK?" Rudy snapped back loudly. He had spent quite a number of days filtering through the witness statements to ultimately design the masterpiece in front of him—a pictorial mapping of the crime scene and possible suspects. He had the rudimentary schematics of the High-Top Lounge as the base of the work, and what looked like a hundred pins of various colors in different combinations stuck to the board with small flags on them. Rudy turned to Steve, "Give me a yellow pin, and name it Holly Bolton." Steve used a felt tip pen in block letters to scrawl the name on the short flag and handed it over.

"Why is she yellow again?" asked Steve,

"Because she was noticed by four other witnesses at the club being within twenty-five feet of the bathroom door at the given time," responded Rudy. "I'm telling you, there is a logic to this. Now, step back and take a look." Steve stepped back and looked, but all he saw was a bunch of colored pins in the wall with tags on them.

"Maybe I just don't have your eye for artistry or something, but what is it that you see?" asked Steve.

Rudy felt quite pleased with himself that he finally had one over on Steve for a change. "Well, I started with a person being a colorless pin if they didn't have any potential involvement in the crime. Then, as there were interactions from the reference material we had, I would change the color to suit a more likely candidate for the one who committed the crime. Don't you see the ebb and flow of the colors here and there? This group had just parted from that crowd over there."

"OK, you're a social genius. What color is guilty?" prodded Steve.

"Oh, you're ruining the moment!" said Rudy, deflated, "But, OK, I used a hot/cold system, so the more red it has, the more likely the person was to be the murderer. And that short list is three names: Drumroll please… Edward Nguyen, Tony Berkshire, and everyone's electronic guru, Levi Mendez."

"Well, you interviewed Mendez and gave him flying colors before. I'd just as soon leave him on the back burner for now since this is a high-profile situation," said Steve. "By the way, how long did it take you to put that thing together?"

"Don't ask," said Rudy, "more time than I'll get credit for."

"Aww," started Steve, "poor Rudy doesn't get an award for his art project. Tell you what, if the murderer turns out to be one of these three, you will get all the accolades for being the biggest brain in the boardroom, OK?"

Rudy perked up with a smile. Then Steve said, "You know, of course, it could have been someone hiding in the bathroom the whole time who wasn't part of the party at all." Rudy looked defeated. "I'm just messing with ya! It wouldn't make sense to sit in hiding the whole day if this is an opportunity killing. Let's start with background records on the three and see if there's anything violent."

"You got it, boss," Rudy said with a fake salute. He turned and started punching keys on the computer to pull up information on the potential suspects. "OK, first one up is Edward Nguyen. The guy has a real estate license, five foot, four inches and 121 pounds according to his driver's license, so I'm not holding my breath on this guy being the physically dominant one of the bunch. But, then again, it doesn't take much to hold a knife." Rudy pointed at the screen, "It says here his adult record is clean, but his juvenile record is sealed. We might want to take a looksie at that one."

"So noted," added Steve, "and the next guy?"

Rudy typed a few keys and the screen changed, "Anthony 'Tony' Berkshire, money management professional by the look of his licenses, six foot one and 185 pounds. This guy seems like a potential, physically, but he has a completely clean record. I can't even find a speeding ticket on him. Maybe he went off his meds or something?"

Steve chided, "Let's hope not taking meds doesn't produce this type of action as a norm, or we'll be way in over our heads with these cases. Let's bring up Mr. Mendez."

"OK," Rudy turned again, "Levi Mendez, no licenses other than a driver's license. Oh, here we go, another sealed juvenile record, but there are a couple of run-ins after his majority for gang-related activities. Nothing that stuck, but contacts were made—nothing recent."

Steve paused before saying, "I think we should bring the first two back in for additional questioning. I'd like to oversee the questioning of both. Then, if we still don't get any leads, we'll request that Mr. Mendez come talk to us at a convenient time.

"Let's go get 'em," said Rudy.

CHAPTER THIRTEEN

------◆·◆·◆------

After classes were let out, Kurt told Terence and Alan to meet him in the school's library, which was located in the center of the main building between the office and administration cubicles and the rest of the classrooms. The library was closed, but since the school was still technically open, the lights were on, just dimmed. They would only have a few minutes before the school's security staff would be making sure there were no students left in the building before they systematically locked it up. Once the three were together, Kurt had them follow him to the southeast corner of the classes, where the Spanish room was located. It was eerily quiet.

Terence whispered, "We're going to get busted if we stay in here too long."

Kurt assured him, "You wanted to know about what's been going on, and I couldn't think of a better place to show you."

Alan looked at him oddly, "In the Spanish room? Why would this be the location we'd need to see it?"

Kurt smiled, put a hand on each of the other guys' shoulders and poof, they were gone.

They materialized in Kurt's bedroom with a whoosh of air, knocking some loose papers around. Kurt dropped his backpack, jumped back into his bed, and put his hands behind his head grinning from ear to ear, "So, what do you think of that?"

No noise came from the boys. They were just staring wide-eyed at each other, then at Kurt, then back at each other again. Then they tried to talk at the same time, making it difficult for Kurt to understand anything.

"Slow down..." Kurt said, "we have lots of time."

Alan started, "Hey, that was cool. Was that the stuff you were keeping secret from us?"

"That's part of it," began Kurt, "There is a lot more to it than that, but I wanted you guys to know about the abilities of my Stone because you're my friends and have always had my back."

"So," ventured Terence, "does this mean we'll be able to have our own Stones eventually that can do stuff like yours does?"

Kurt shook his head and told the guys about the backstory of angel DNA and how only those with certain DNA markers can hold or use the Stones.

"Bummer," was all Terence gave back.

"Hey," Alan began, "you know what's the second-best thing to having superpowers?"

"No," said Terence.

"Having your best friend have superpowers! Now think about it," Alan finished.

Kurt smiled hearing Alan say that. He wasn't sure how the guys would take it, but he hoped they would still be his friends. Kurt explained his limitations on traveling and also explained his ability to have extra strength when he needed it.

"Oh, so that's how you threw Mackey in the fountain," concluded Terence.

"Yup, and about that… I'm sorry for doing that. I shouldn't have done it that way. I was more of a bully than he ever was. I'm hoping he'll forgive me for what I did," Kurt said remorsefully.

"But that makes you the strongest guy in the city, maybe even the state or the planet," said Alan. "You could make millions in football or baseball!"

"No, that's not what I have this ability for," corrected Kurt. "I have this for a reason, which isn't totally clear so far, but it's not for me to make extra money on. There's something more honorable about it. Also, if I start showing my gifts, it'll make it dangerous for the other people who have Stones. It could make it dangerous for my friends if someone wanted to get to me. It's best this stays a secret."

"But, hey, could you zap us to our own rooms, too?" asked Terence. "You've been there before."

"True, but I haven't been there enough times to really know it like the back of my hand. I would have to have some kind of pattern or anchor to get me there," answered Kurt. "It's hard to explain. Wait a second, I have an idea."

Kurt rummaged through his top dresser drawer and found a couple of bandanas he had from camping long ago. He unwrapped them, got out his thick permanent marker, and in block letters wrote each of their names on the cloths before handing them out. "Now, put these in your room, maybe under your bed or somewhere no one is going to pick it up and move it around, and I'll be able to zap into your rooms later."

Alan and Terence were jumping with excitement. Alan started, "That's so cool. We could have sleep-overs and our parents would never know!"

Terence picked up his backpack and was already heading for the door when he said, "I'm the first one to try it. Give me five minutes to get to my room."

"Not if I get to my room first," called out Alan doing the same thing. All the boys were laughing and having fun. It was like the best game of hide and seek!

Kurt sat down and watched his clock for five minutes to pass. It seemed like an eternity, but eventually it hit and with a whoosh, he disappeared....

....and was suddenly in Terence's room, with a bewildered cat jumping out of the way, hissing.

"That is so awesome!" said Terence, "OK, let's go get Alan."

Kurt put his hand on Terence's shoulder and a few seconds later, they were in Alan's bedroom, getting ready to sit down and get comfortable.

"You know, someone could get used to this type of travel," said Terence with a smarmy sound in his voice.

"Yeah, but I'm not going to abuse it. I wanted to test out that I could do what I thought I could, and I did. Best to keep up appearances of being normal so I don't get caught," said Kurt, "but it is fun, isn't it? I'll have to be careful. Being strong is one thing and can be explained away, but teleportation is not something most people would understand."

"Hey," started Alan, "I didn't get stuck with any homework today and it's not your day for karate class, right?"

Kurt nodded.

"So, what say we go down to the mall and check out the new 3-D game they just put in? Yeah, the time traveler one."

"Cool, those holograms make me feel like I'm crossing my

eyes," said Terence, "but they look like they're right there and can be touched. It's awesome."

The guys got their gear in order, and to the correct apartments. Then, they ventured out to Second Street, and down Broadway until they came to Parkway Vista Mall.

Upon arriving at the mall, there were quite a few Mendez Micro-Tech trucks in the parking lot. When they got closer, they could see the signs on the doors telling everyone about how the stores were being rewired for a new point of sale method that was going to be introduced shortly. Parkway Vista Mall bragged they were the first mall chain to have the test market. If successful, the model would expand to the whole county of San Diego as the test market. All the stores in all the malls of the East Meadow Corporation in the county were being fitted with this technology.

"Wow," said Alan, "I wonder what it's going to be. I've seen the ads for the Producer. That guy must be smart and rich. I asked my dad about getting a Producer, but he said something about it's just a fad, and it'll come and go."

"Hey, Kurt," prodded Terence, "any chance we get home without having to walk?"

"We'll see," said Kurt, "remember what I said about overusing it. It's asking to get caught."

They walked in to find everything fairly normal, except every register and checkout counter had a Mendez MicroTech technician. Upon closer inspection, it seemed they were installing these black plastic squares that were ninety degrees to each other at the edge, so they'd fit on the corner of the sales counter. There was a slight indentation of a right hand in the plastic so that a person would comfortably set their hand into that position and the fingers and thumb would line up appropriately. Mendez MicroTech's logo was apparent in the hand indentation between the thumb and forefinger, and again at the lower-right corner of the square.

Alan was feeling curious and asked one of the technicians about the apparatus.

"Hey, I just install the thing. I don't know how it works," said the technician, "but they said there's going to be something about it in the news tonight. A breakthrough in technology or something. We have to get all of these things up and going before the ten o'clock local news hits, or it's our butts."

Kurt noticed when the technician was testing the plastic squares, he was waving his hand in front of the square and the red light would turn green. The technician seemed satisfied when this happened and would move along to the next function. Kurt figured it was some type of swipe technology like his cell phone had, and thought, good luck, that was a pain in the neck to do on his phone. The boys made their way to the video game section of the mall and spent the rest of the afternoon playing in the arcade.

* * *

Steve never passed up getting together with the other detectives at the Broken Clock Tavern after work, when they invited him. Not only did it get rid of feeling alone for a few hours, but he could always use his Stone to cure the alcohol from his system before he needed to drive home. That was one of the nice, albeit selfish, perks of this particular Stone. He walked into the tavern hearing his name called a few times as he made his way down to sit next to Rudy and Tim at one of the tables.

San Diego was well renowned for being one of the craft brew capitals of the northern hemisphere. This bar wasn't shy in displaying that with fifty-six beers on tap. Steve signaled the bartender to bring him a pint and some appetizers while he listened to the varied conversations in the room about beer, hops, malt, work, and more. The employees knew their stuff about the microbrew industry and would be able to answer any questions on the spot. The dartboard and shuffleboard were untouched, more for show than for use in recent years. Individual digital screens were available at every location with several games going on while people were having their drinks—some playing trivia, others playing solitaire.

When Steve sat down, Tim was absently poking at the screen in front of him. Rudy wasn't paying any attention to his, as he was more concerned with viewing the waitress who just walked past. He turned back and said, "Dang, if I were fifteen years younger…"

"…and a whole lot prettier," Steve added laughing. Tim was still glued to his screen intensely. From the looks of it, he was probably doing well in the trivia game with the other patrons in the bar. A quick glance over to the scoreboard above the tap handles showed Tim and another player neck and neck. The other player was anonymous, so guessing who was up that high was part of the fun. Everyone was looking around for someone who appeared tense or determined, but there were just cold poker faces and knowing grins. Finally, after the last question was sent over the screens, Tim lost out by one point.

"Oh!!" shouted Tim covering his face with his hands, "I was so close! Who was the one who beat me?" He bobbed his head back and forth to see if anyone would fess up, but no one did. Once he was settled down and moping to himself, Steve caught the bartender's eye and the bartender put up one hand to cover the other and pointed at a booth near the back. A family was eating there with a young teenager, a furtive grin on his face and playing with the console in front of him. Steve gave the "really?" look, and the bartender confirmed. Oh, this was going to fuel plenty of fun later for razzing Tim, thought Steve.

"Well, what'd you think of Eddie Nguyen today in interrogation?" opened Rudy.

"Hey, this is after hours. We'll talk about work during work hours, OK?" countered Steve. "So, how are Carla and the kids?"

Rudy looked distressed. "Carla is doing great, but trying to keep up with four kids is a nightmare. It seems someone is always going somewhere at the exact same time on the other side of town and it's always urgent. The only time I know where all of them are is when they're in bed."

Steve laughed, "But, you wouldn't have it any other way."

"No, I supposed not," Rudy continued, "Mikey is a senior now, so he's looking to intern soon to fulfill his community experience requirements to graduate. He's looking into engineering, so I'll be passing around the hat for college donations shortly."

"Hey, maybe you can get him an internship over at Mendez MicroTech, since we're probably going to have to go by there anyway," Steve joked.

"You think?" Rudy looked genuinely intrigued by the idea.

"I wouldn't mix business with family," Steve countered, "but, if it comes up, we can certainly entertain the idea."

"Well, speak of the devil..." started Tim, as he pointed up at the TV display. The local KFNT news had come on and the anchors were speaking with a photo of Levi Mendez in the background. Rudy yelled for the bartender to turn up the volume on the set.

"...and the shopping center chain, East Meadow Corporation, has teamed up to provide a new way of shopping," said the TV anchor. "And now, out to our live correspondent at the Parkway Vista

Mall."

The scene cut to the front of a sales counter at one of the stores in Parkway Vista Mall, showing the reporter and several patrons standing around waving their hands in greetings to the camera.

"This is Sid Price with KFNT news at Parkway Vista Mall, live to show some of the new features and technology proposed by this new venture between two very large companies. As you can see, all you have to do to process a transaction is wave your right hand in front of this device. It will read the implant talked about in our last segment, and give you complete control of your finances at the shopping center."

The reporter turned to look at someone demonstrating this swipe and continued, "Your PIN is still required at this time to verify the transaction, but they said they are working on complete encrypted validation to do away with the need for PIN numbers, eventually. All the power of shopping in the palm of your hand. Implant injections will begin for free next week at the MicroTech facilities. Back to you in the studio, this is Sid Price, signing out."

"Whoa, that's a jump in tech!" said one of the anchors.

"Not really," said another, "We've had RFID technology for some time now. It was just a matter of making it marketable—making it palatable to the people. I think what Levi Mendez is doing might just bridge that gap."

"Wait," the other anchor said covering his ear, "I've just got new details in. Mendez MicroTech and East Meadows Corp are offering $1,000 in credit to the first 1,000 people who get the implant for shopping. After that, it's free as before, but wait .... they're going to give a forty percent discount on all items purchased with the implant for the first week of shopping in any East Meadows Mall!"

The other anchor mimed an excited face to the camera while the other anchor continued, "and that includes purchases in the food courts. Wow, what a deal! I think I'll have to get one."

"You and me, both!" said the other anchor. "We're lucky to be living in San Diego for this trial run. If everything pans out, this may very well be the way of the future. Levi Mendez was unavailable for a statement."

"How odd?" mumbled Steve, "Biggest breakthrough in the guy's business and he's unavailable for a statement?"

"Oh, you know what those rich, fat cats are like! They all have that germ-a-phobia and stuff," bantered Rudy. "He'll show his face soon enough. Maybe he went in for a nose job or something. But, I doubt he's going to see us in person anytime soon with all that going on. We might be able to get a phone call in."

"Call his office in the morning to try to set something up. Time to be heading outta here. We do have to work tomorrow," said Steve.

Rudy nodded. Steve stood up, put his hand on Rudy's shoulder, and wiped out most of the alcohol from his system till he was under the limit. He went around the room, saying his farewells, shaking hands and doing the same thing to the other coworkers without their knowledge. Depending on what he saw left on the table, he'd adjust to make sure no one would leave with too much alcohol in their system, assuming it was the last call. He did this regularly, and there had never been an accident or incident at his precinct as long as he'd been using this technique. No one ever said anything about suddenly being more aware—they were always pleased and made it to work the next day without a hangover.

Steve thought about his son while walking to his car. *I may not be able to cure the world, he pondered, but I'm going to make sure I can keep my friends alive—I'll do my part.* He got into his car, started the engine, and drove home.

CHAPTER FOURTEEN

I t was almost 4:00 p.m. the following day when Levi Mendez sat down in his conference room, opposite his two attorneys, with a multi-line phone speaker in the center of the table. The room was unnecessarily large, but it was central and intentionally chosen for passersby to overhear the conversations. Prior to making any phone calls, Levi stuck his hand out to one of his attorneys.

"Would you mind lending me your phone for a text I need to send?" inquired Levi, "I left my phone in my office accidentally."

The attorney barely showed any change in expression while placing his hand in his pocket to take out his phone and hand it over. With the prices they were charging, he could keep the phone if he wanted to. Levi punched in a phone number, then texted, "We're in a meeting for a couple of hours. Start the project and update me later." He then handed the phone back.

"Thank you. Now is everyone ready? Here it goes..." Levi dialed a phone number on the table phone and waited for the pickup. "Hi,

Levi Mendez to speak with Detective Bailey…Yes, he's expecting my call…I'll hold."

After a few moments a click and a voice sounded, "Hi, Mr. Mendez. This is Detective Bailey. Thank you for returning our call. I was hoping to ask you a few questions about the event in the Top-Hat Bar a few weeks ago?"

"Detective Bailey, I would be happy to answer your questions. Please be aware that my attorneys are present, and they will likely intervene if they feel my rights are being pushed or bruised in any way."

"I understand, Mr. Mendez. However, you are not under arrest. We are just looking for answers at this time to further conduct our investigation. Now, I have it on your statement here that you attempted to enter the bathroom, but it was locked, so you returned to where you were before?"

"Detective Bailey, if you're reading my file, it clearly would state that I found the door locked to the bathroom, so I left the bar in order to go back to my office to use the restroom. Since my office is only a five-minute drive from that location, it seemed like a good choice. I was also finished with being at the bar for that evening," responded Mendez.

"Oh, yes, I see here now, that is what you said in your statement. The problem I have is that I have one witness who said they saw you enter the restroom which you said was locked," replied Bailey.

"Then, I would say that the other person wasn't sober enough to recall correctly, or has me mixed up with someone else. I made one other trip to the bathroom earlier. Perhaps your witness is referring to seeing me at that time," said Mendez.

Bailey clarified, "Even if it would be considered hearsay in a court, I must take it seriously during an investigation. One last question and then I'll let you get back to your busy schedule. Did you happen to notice anyone ahead of you before you reached the bathroom who entered before you? Maybe someone who could have locked it prior to your reaching the door?"

"As mentioned in my statement, I didn't see anyone go in or out prior to my getting to the door. Once I found it was locked, I turned around, left, and that was that," responded Levi.

"Well, I appreciate your time. Good evening."

"Goodbye."

Click.

"Well," began Levi, "I guess I didn't need you guys after all. I think we can call it a day."

Getting up first, he smiled and jetted towards the door before the attorneys were through putting their things away. As he was walking down the hall, he felt a buzzing in his jacket pocket. He pulled out his phone he had had the whole time and checked the incoming text, "I just missed your phone call ten minutes ago. Call me back when you have a moment. Nothing urgent—everything good here."

Levi smiled. That meant everything went according to plan. *I will get to relax without law enforcement harassing me*, he thought. There was a spring in his step as he entered his office and closed the door.

* * *

The weekend had finally arrived, and Kurt was debating going over to Bill Mackey's house to apologize for what he had done to him in front of all the school kids. He had had an opportunity to talk to him at school, but the added pressure of others watching Mackey act out a fight or flight wasn't the situation he wanted. He decided to wait until Saturday. If Mackey didn't want to talk, all he would probably get was a slammed door in his face.

After putting on his running shoes, he made his way out of the complex and down a couple of blocks to where he knew Mackey lived. Along the way, he memorized what he was going to say. He'd be prepared for the door to shut, so he'd have to have something pivotal to say within the first few seconds. Maybe he should have waited till the sun tilted further down, but knew his courage might dwindle. He left just after noon, with the sun high in the sky.

Reciting the words to himself, he walked to Mackey's front door and rang the bell. He heard someone walking slowly to the door and fumble with the lock. The door cracked open and a blast of alcohol odor tumbled out, attacking Kurt's nose. It appeared to be Mackey's dad answering the door. His hair was a mussed mass of grey and black. His five o'clock shadow was four days overdue. When he opened his mouth to grunt out a guttural sound to pass for a greeting of some kind, Kurt could see most of his teeth were missing and the ones which were left were decaying badly. He took the moment of Kurt's silence to tilt back another guzzle of his beer before saying, "Well….?"

"I was hoping to speak with Billy if I could," Kurt barely got out through the stench.

"Well, Billy isn't seeing anyone right now," responded his dad tauntingly.

His dad was trying to cover most of the open door with his body, but there was a sliver visible into the living room. He could see Bill peeking from around the sofa. Aside from the top of the sling near his neck, Kurt could see a shiner on one of his eyes. Kurt knew there had been no damage done to his face during their incident at school.

"I see. I will try again another time," said Kurt.

"Yeah, you do that," Mackey's dad's voice dripped with sarcasm.

The door slammed in front of him. He stood there for a minute, not knowing exactly what to do. Then, he heard Mackey's dad yelling at Billy at the top of his lungs. He could barely make out what was being said as the words were slurred and annunciated incorrectly. He heard a slap and a boy crying. That's all Kurt could take—he knew he couldn't use his abilities in public, but he knew someone he could call for help.

He ran out of the yard and down the street a bit, then got out his phone and called Detective Bailey directly. He was only supposed to do this in emergencies, and this counted as one. Steve answered the phone after a couple of rings. Kurt filled him in on what was going on and why he was there.

"I'm glad you didn't take it into your own hands. This is definitely something for the authorities to handle. That's out of my jurisdiction, but I have a friend on the El Cajon PD who can meet us over there. Give me the address and I'll call him on my way," responded Steve. Kurt passed along the address and was told to wait at a distance from the home until he got there.

An El Cajon PD cruiser showed up first, no lights flashing. He pulled up to the curb and asked, "Are you Kurt?"

When Kurt responded in the affirmative, the officer said, "I'm Officer Owens. Hold tight and Steve should be here any minute." Another five minutes passed and then Steve's car pulled up. With both cars parked, the officer and detective joined Kurt in walking back to the Mackey residence.

Steve and Officer Owens walked up the couple of stairs to the landing before the door, Kurt a step behind in tow. Steve was about to knock, when he heard a man screaming at someone inside the door. Officer Owens knocked loudly on the door. Kurt looked at the two of them side by side and knew he wouldn't want to be Bill's dad right now. Aside from Steve being six foot, two inches tall, Officer Owens was built like a barrel and only a couple of inches shorter than Steve.

The sound of the locks being undone on the inside occurred again, and the door cracked as a yell started from the dad's lips, "I told you he isn't avial.l.l.." His voice stopped when he realized there were two giants looking down at his much shorter and gaunter frame. Owens was in his beat uniform, and Steve was wearing his regular detective attire with his badge clipped to his belt. Bill's dad's eyes grew very wide and he asked, "Yes, officers, what can I do for you?"

Since it was his jurisdiction, Officer Owens did all the talking, "We heard there may have been something going on at this address and we came to take a look. May we come in?"

"Um, er, don't you need a warrant for that?" stammered his dad.

"Not if you give me permission to enter. You wouldn't be hiding anything, would you?"

"No, of course not. I suppose you can come in," he responded.

After both entered, followed by Kurt, they glanced around. It appeared the home had not been picked up in some time. A thick layer of dust was accumulated on nearly every shelf, lamp hood, and knick-knack. The couch and chair had duct tape, assumedly to close up tears or holes in the fabric. There were various stains on the carpeting which didn't require much guessing.

"I believe your son is here?" asked Officer Owens.

"Yes, but he's gone to take a nap," his dad quickly responded.

"Does he always nap at the top of the stairs with his eyes open?" asked Owens.

His dad looked around to see Bill curiously looking in on what was going on. His dad signaled him to come down.

The detective and officer looked at the beat-up kid, and the officer asked, "Where did you get that black eye?"

"From him!" Billy pointed directly at Kurt.

"Really? From this little guy here? He must be at least a foot shorter than you! I bet you're going to tell me next that he broke your arm, too," said Steve, jumping into the conversation.

"Well, yes, he did!" said Mackey.

"You're kidding! There's no way! Why are you covering for someone else?" Steve asked.

"I-I-I'm n-n-not," Billy stuttered. This was too much. He began to let the tears stream down his face.

"Stop being such a sissy!" his dad piped in, "no wonder that little kid could beat you up. You're such a baby."

"Hey, that's enough of that," Officer Owens said. He went over and told Mackey's dad to put his hands behind his back. He started putting on handcuffs and telling him, "I'm arresting you on child endangerment for being as intoxicated as you are, and child abuse in the form of physical and mental abuse. We'll get Billy's statement when you aren't around." He finished with the Miranda rights then he turned to Billy, "You're going to be safe now. Is your mom home?"

Bill shook his head, "She doesn't live with us."

"Gather some of your things. A couple days' change of clothing, and we'll take you down to the Center until we can get things straightened out. We can't leave you here by yourself," said Steve.

Billy got his things together and joined them back in the living room. They all left together—Officer Owens taking Billy's dad in his patrol car, and Steve taking Kurt and Billy in his car. Steve started driving to the Pulaski Center.

Sometime along the way, Billy turned to Kurt, "Why were you at my house anyways?" His face was still streaked with dried tears and his eyes were swollen red, "You've really jacked up my life, you know."

"I was there to apologize for what I did to you, and for how I embarrassed you. I didn't realize at the time, but I was being a worse bully than you were being to me. It really bothers me that I broke your arm," replied Kurt. "When I heard the yelling and then saw the black eye, I knew something was wrong. I did what I did to protect you, not to hurt you more."

"But look at what you're doing. At least before, I lived at my home and went to school. Now I'll be stuck in Juvenile Hall until I'm old enough to get out. How is that fair to me?" Mackey shot back.

"You won't be anyone's punching bag ever again," said Kurt, "that's the best I could do." He turned and sat back to watch the road the rest of the way. Mackey just stared down, waiting for the inevitable.

They arrived at the Center without incident and Kurt was instructed to wait in the lobby so Steve could escort Billy to the intake personnel, a tall man with a beard who looked kindly at Mackey, "We know this isn't an easy day for you. After we set you up, we'll get some food and maybe you can find a favorite movie to watch from our library. Why don't you look over this list now to see if there's anything you might be interested in?"

The man with the beard handed a clipboard to Steve to fill out a couple of forms. Billy was silent, slumping down in the chair, looking more like a lost kid and less like the school-yard bully.

Once Steve was done with the forms, he turned to Billy. "Hey, I know I'm not your favorite person on the planet right now," started Steve, "but hear me out for a minute. We're here to make sure you don't get beat up again. It's not your fault, and it's not your place to be a stress reliever for your dad. I know you're going to wonder for a while if this is worse than what you were going through before. I promise, I will keep an eye on things. I'm not going to let the system eat you up. Kurt is a good kid, and he was the one that was looking out for you. Now I'll be looking out for you, too.

Billy just nodded his head in silence. He was trying his hardest not to cry. He'd never felt so alone, but he was appreciative the detective was taking an interest in him.

"But, why me?" asked Billy Mackey.

"Because I think kids should get a chance to live out their lives without the crap sandwich that life throws at them sometimes. And, you know, my parents are also both gone, so we're along the same stripe and have to look out for our kind," Steve answered in a supportive tone. "The people here at the Center will get you situated with meals and a room. Once you get yourself on a schedule, they'll let you make a phone call. If you want, you can call me. Here's my card."

Steve knew he had to get Kurt back before his dad got home so he stood up and handed the forms back to the friendly bearded man.

"Listen, I've got to go now, but this isn't the last we'll see each other. You're not alone."

Billy tried to put on a brave face in front of this unlikely rescuer. He nodded at Steve as he took the business card from Steve's outstretched hand, "I won't throw it away, you know." Steve smiled inside a bit. It was a lot for a kid like Mackey to be able to trust any adult. Steve wished he could do more, but he knew the people at the Center, and felt confident Billy was now in safe hands.

"Take care, kid," he said with a firm pat to Billy's shoulders, "It's going to be OK."

He turned from Mackey and went back up the hallway to the lobby where Kurt was waiting. After saying it was time to go home, Kurt reminded him that he could get back anytime needed. "Hey, let's stop by your place. I've never been there," suggested Kurt. "Maybe you can show me that book again."

"OK, for a few minutes, then you gotta skedaddle," Steve replied.

They arrived at his home a few minutes later. Kurt was antsy to see the book again and followed Steve inside. He closely took note of things in Steve's house if he ever needed to get here in an emergency. He found a few things he could memorize, and locked them into his brain for later use. He even crossed the room when Steve was occupied and zapped himself back to the first part of the room he had memorized, to verify he had it down. He was getting much better at memorizing locations. Picturing them was becoming easier. He was sure the Stone had something to do with it, but he was all on board for the help.

Steve brought out the ancient book, unwrapped it, and laid it on the table. He flipped to the page showing the Enochian writing and the circle with the green hue. The rest of the page was empty. He handed a felt-tipped pen, a quite fancy one at that, to Kurt and cleared his throat. "You are the bearer of the Stone of Gabriel. You are the curator of its mysteries and effects. You may write as little or as much information as you see fit to provide on these pages for the next in each of our lineages to reflect upon."

"But, how would they know to come to you?" Kurt asked.

"Ahh, an excellent question, but not one you have to worry about," Steve began, "Others have been notified of your recovery of the Stone and are now preparing a book for you. It will have all the information available from the Stones in the eastern hemisphere. It will also have my Stone's information because we share information. I'm trying to keep my book as current as possible, so anything you're willing to write in my book would be appreciated. You have the freedom to write whatever you wish into your own book for your next predecessor."

"Oh, I see. And you want me to write in it instead of my telling you what's what and having you write it?"

"No, I'd rather have the author's hand to the note. You can look at the other pages for ideas of what to write if you're unsure," said Steve.

Kurt flipped back and forth between the pages, reading only the English portions at the bottom of the pages. He got a sense of what he was going to write, then turned back to Gabriel's page. He was about to start writing on the bottom of the page when Steve gently picked up his hand and guided it to the very next line under the Enochian writing. Kurt was in awe. His was going to be the first writing in the highest position. He had better make it good. He slowed down and printed his very best:

Stone of Gabriel: Found on a Native American reservation north of San Diego County in a dry riverbed with hundreds of river rocks. Has the ability of strength and teleportation. Teleportation takes a while to get the hang of it.

He blew on what he had written to make sure the ink was dry, then closed the book. He handed the book back to Steve. While Steve was busy putting it back in the safe, Kurt took the opportunity to look around a bit. He noticed a lot of pictures in the hallway and walked over for a look. It appeared there were fingerprints on the glass over every picture's face. He could still see enough to make out Steve's family before the tragedy. He started walking back to the kitchen area to say goodbye to Steve when he passed the little table with the bowl where Bailey threw his keys. Kurt saw two familiar coins Steve must have tossed in. He picked up the son's coin again and marveled at the detail in Christopher's face. He flipped the coin over and looked at the intricate detail of the angel's wings, the crucifix, and the perfect edges of the font showing Matthew 19:14. He heard Steve approaching and dropped the coin back into the bowl.

"Hey, it's getting late. You don't want to pop up with your dad staring at you," said Steve. He knew that Kurt's dad was picking up extra shifts on Saturdays to make ends meet, but he'd be home by six.

"No, that might be a bit hard to explain," smiled Kurt. "I'll catch you next time." He stuck his hand out for Steve to shake it. But, just as Steve was about to grab it, he pulled his hand to his head, "Too slow…" He smiled, and then popped out of the room.

CHAPTER FIFTEEN

About a half hour later, when Steve was just getting relaxed and ready to watch a bit of evening TV, his phone started ringing. He picked it up and heard dispatch telling him he had another crime scene to inspect. He knew Rudy was getting the same call, so he got dressed again and drove to the site, twenty-five minutes north of his house. It was not in his jurisdiction, but everyone knew he was to be notified if anything like the previous murders happened again.

Because he was being called to an unincorporated city, the San Diego Sheriff's Department had the scene under control. The house was indistinct from several of the others in the neighborhood. Steve walked in the door to find the crime scene unit taping off certain areas, dusting for prints, and performing half a dozen other procedures. The coroner was just finishing with the body when Steve walked up.

"Hi, Detective Steve Bailey, SDPD Homicide. Do you have any

information about the victim?" asked Steve.

"Actually, quite a bit I've noticed," started the coroner. "To start things off, the reason they called you in."

Rudy was walking up with Steve's cup of coffee just as the coroner lifted the body's shirt to show the phosphorescent writing on the abdomen. This time, it seemed to be some type of math equation. '3-2=1', however there were wavy lines above and below the '2'.

The coroner continued, "I'm stumped as to what the wavy lines represent. They appear to be waves. The victim's name is Ernesto Garcia, thirty-seven."

Steve did all he could to keep his face straight. He knew exactly what that equation meant, and knew it was meant for him specifically. '3-2=1' was referring to his family of three, two being killed in the house fire, and leaving just himself behind. Now he knew for sure that the demon who did this knew him. The evidence all pointed to the arsonist who was never caught, the one who burned Steve's house, and was possessed by this very demon. Although, this scene didn't reflect the savagery of the bar murder. It seemed as though the demon was reveling in the blood at the nightclub. But at this location, there was very little blood other than a small amount right around the body.

"Anything else?" asked Bailey.

"Yes," began the coroner, "there are scuff marks along the back of the shoes, meaning the body was dragged at some point. Because of the lack of blood, I'm thinking this may not have been the original murder location."

If the perpetrator had to drag the body, he couldn't be that strong. This victim wasn't more than 150 pounds. *The bodies at the last location were moved around quite easily*, thought Steve.

"Do you know the time of death?" inquired Bailey.

"The temperature of the liver and ambient temperature of this room indicates that the victim was killed sometime around 3 p.m. to 5 p.m. yesterday, probably leaning on the earlier of that time frame," responded the coroner.

"Who found the body?"

"You'll have to talk to one of the deputies about that," the coroner returned.

Steven thanked him and then looked for one of the officers to question. On his way, he stopped one of the CSU team and asked if they had found the murder weapon. The team member said, "Yes, strangely enough, the perp left it right outside the front door for anyone to find."

Well, at least that's consistent, thought Steve. Maybe he just didn't have enough data, or the perp was evolving. He took pictures with his phone for quick reference and went to talk to the nearest deputy.

"Deputy Barnes, do you happen to know who found the victim?" asked Steve.

Barnes, not looking up from the notes he was writing, tilted his head towards the hallway leading to the kitchen. Steve headed down that way and found a woman sitting at the kitchen table with a grey blanket—definitely sheriff issue—over her shaking shoulders, and a female deputy sitting nearby, jotting down information. Detective Bailey showed his badge to the deputy, who got up and came over to him, keeping a bit of distance from the shaken woman, but not too far out of reach to where she'd feel alone.

"This is Karen Oberlies, a real estate agent, and the agent for this home which is vacant due to foreclosure," the deputy said in hushed tones, "She came by the property today because she was going to prep it for potential buyers when she found the body. She didn't touch anything—she immediately dialed 911 and waited outside."

Steve nodded and took notes while the deputy spoke. He passed her his card and told her if anything else comes up to give him a call. Then he walked back to the living room where Rudy was asking questions of the CSU team. He motioned for Rudy to hurry up. Once Rudy joined him, he said, "I'd like to get back to the precinct to run our suspects' phones to find out what towers they were near between three and five yesterday."

"Yeah, then we can rule out their phones as suspects," Rudy chuckled.

"OK, I know it's a longshot, but it's at least worth a try. Who knows, maybe the perp was dumb enough to keep his phone with him during the murder," said Steve.

"I'll meet you down there in a bit. I just want to finish a few questions here," said Rudy.

Steve nodded and left. He drove back to the precinct and started on the cell phone triangulations. Rudy arrived just as he was finishing the first one on Eddie Nguyen, who appeared to have been at his place of employment during those hours. Rudy started on Tony Berkshire and found he was apparently stuck in traffic for most of that time, or at his home towards the end of the time frame, neither of which would put him within half an hour's drive from the crime scene. Lastly, Steve ran it for Levi Mendez, hoping something would come of it. Unfortunately, the scan showed Levi's phone to be at his business for the entire time, matching the conference call Levi had had with him. Steve struck his fist on the table.

"Can't catch a break!" exclaimed Bailey.

"Hold up, Steve. It's not all that bad. You've overlooked one small detail," said Rudy with a grin.

"Yeah? What's that?"

Rudy straightened his collar, cleared his throat and began, "If the vacant home was in fact a dump site for the body and not the original murder location, which is substantiated by the lack of blood and the scuffs on the back of the victim's shoes, then why would the murder weapon be outside the dump site? The perp always tosses it outside his kill site."

"That's it! It's been bugging me with all these things not adding up. It seems like this one is completely off, but still similar to the other homicides. And, I'm including the one from Barry Finley, since that one looked similar, also. This one today looked staged, like someone was told what to do but not shown the particulars," gathered Steve.

"Which puts us back at square one as far as who might be behind the killings," pointed out Rudy.

"Not necessarily," Steve answered back. "The only reason someone would have someone *else* stage a murder would be to throw us off the tracks of who might actually be the mastermind. We must have been getting close to something. I think your shortlist has the perp on it and we rattled some cages. I know who my money is on."

"Really? You think he'd throw away all that wealth and fame to murder some people and potentially get caught?" rebounded Rudy.

"I think," Steve began, "that murder is a sickness deep down in one's heart. I don't think the perp cares how much money or what kind of fame he has. I think he wants to have the power over another life as the ultimate control. And these gimmicks on the abdomen of the victims further allude to the idea that he's somehow smarter than we are, and in a more powerful position."

"Almost like a Dr. Jekyll and Mr. Hyde situation, huh?" asked Rudy.

"Quite similar, but this nut job doesn't require a potion to make it happen. He was either born with his wires crossed badly or his environment was so horrible that this is normal for him. Depends if you believe nature or nurture. Personally, I think it's a bit of both," answered Steve. "But, usually there's something that starts it off—some kind of trigger. I think if we can figure that out, we might be closer to the trail of our perp."

"Well, it's getting late. If I want any chance of seeing my family before they're asleep, I better head out," said Rudy.

"Not a problem. I'm going to go over some things here for a bit. I'll see you Monday morning unless something else pops up," said Steve.

Rudy gathered his belongings and left, leaving Steve scratching his head and fanning through file after file.

* * *

"Hey, Dad! Hurry up! The game is about to start!" Kurt yelled from the living room.

It was Sunday morning, and the professional football games were about to be televised—a sacred time for father and son to vegetate in front of the TV.

"One second," his dad yelled back, "I'm almost done with the chips and dip."

Mr. Palmer came around the corner a minute later with a big bag of chips, a plastic bowl of dip, and a six-pack of soda.

"Sorry, Dad, your team is going dowwwwnnn today!"

"Oh, yeah? We'll see about that." They each had their team jerseys on, and this was one of the few times that their favorite teams got to play each other since they were in different conferences.

On the screen, one of the team's coaches was leading a small prayer group with a few of the players on the sideline before the game started. It sparked a question in Kurt, "Dad, why don't we go to church?"

The question seemed almost a physical blow to his dad. Mr. Palmer's head dropped to his hands and he let out a long breath. He turned off the TV set and turned toward Kurt, inhaling to steady himself.

"B-b-b-ut..." Kurt started, then saw the look in his dad's eyes and left it alone. This was something very serious to him—he could tell from that look—not something to challenge, just to listen.

"What is it, Dad?" asked Kurt when he gathered enough nerve to broach the question.

The happiness he usually saw in his dad's eyes was awash with futility and frustration. His dad began, "I've never talked about this, because it's all tied together. But you're old enough now and deserve to hear everything."

He got up and paced a little bit before turning around and saying, "Try to understand that this is something very difficult for me to talk about. How much do you remember of your mother?"

Kurt said, "Not much. I was too young to remember much. I can remember her holding me and brushing my hair, but not much else." Kurt started to get nervous about what was going to come next.

His dad quietly sat down next to him and started, "It's hard to begin with the first time I met your mom—since I don't recall which time it was. My dad, being in the military, moved around quite a bit. We'd move from here to Newport Beach, out to Perris, and back again. I can't tell you the number of schools I attended before grad-uating. But somehow, every time we were stationed in San Diego, I would go to school, and there she was."

Kurt sat up a little closer. He'd never heard this story before and was quite interested.

Mr. Palmer continued, "We started dating in high school when my dad was finally placed in San Diego permanently before his retirement. I felt like everything was lined up and perfect. She was the most beautiful woman I had ever met." Mr. Palmer's expression lightened as he thought of better times.

"We were inseparable," he continued, "I was yin to her yang. After high school, we both went to the same junior college. I ended up having to go to a trade school, but your mom continued and got her teaching credentials. It was shortly after graduation that we were married. Everything was falling into place like we thought it would. A few years later you were born, my pride and joy." He gave Kurt a light punch on the shoulder.

Kurt feigned injury while Mr. Palmer continued, "It was shortly after that when things started to change. By no means do I think it's related to the pregnancy, but for the next few years certain things about her personality started to show that there was something going on. She would talk about seeing things in other people's faces. There was a history in her family of some type of dementia, but it usually started much earlier and resulted in institutionalization. I didn't know what to do, so I started taking her to specialists."

Mr. Palmer's head dropped into his hand and he didn't talk for some time. It looked as if he were struggling with the next words.

"Psychology and psychiatry don't always have the answers we need. They pumped her full of psychoactive medication, hoping to offset the visions. They even tried shock therapy. No, not like the kind you've seen on TV. Everything they tried…she would still see these distortions in some people's faces. She was fading away before my eyes to a husk of what she once was. Luckily, my mom was able to help me out with you while this was going on. But…"

"What is it, Dad?" asked Kurt.

His dad calmed himself. "I prayed every second I could spare for help from above for her. She never got better—it only got worse. No one is going to fess up whether she overdosed on her meds or the staff screwed up, but one night it was over. I had balled up all the anger inside of me and the frustration and let it out towards God for letting this happen to the most perfect woman I had ever met. Because of this, I've never been able to walk into a church again."

Kurt's eyes were filled with tears, feeling for his dad what must have been torture. He knew what his mom must've seen was the faces of the demons, and she couldn't describe it or have anyone around to explain what it was. He knew if he tried to explain this to his dad right now, his dad would think he was just making things up to make him feel better. It was probably best to let it alone.

But he was thankful for running into Detective Bailey who explained to him what those things were, or he might have ended up in the same situation. He didn't want to complicate his dad's life any further than it already was. Kurt settled for giving his dad a welcomed hug. The game was a distant memory.

CHAPTER SIXTEEN

I t was Monday after school when Kurt walked up to the martial arts studio and knocked on the glass window, hoping Bonnie would answer. He waited a minute and knocked again. Peering through the glass, he could see the lights were out and the alarm was still blinking. Nobody had been by today yet. He got out his phone and texted Detective Bailey hoping he might know something.

A couple of minutes later, his phone rang, and Detective Bailey was on the line, "Hey, kiddo. Sorry. We were supposed to be back in time to pick you up and bring you here. We're working on another training session for you, and just now finished. We'll be there in about twenty minutes if you want to hang around."

"I have one better for you," answered back Kurt. "Are you carrying your coins that you showed me the other day at your house?"

"I have them," Steve replied.

"Then go somewhere no one else is and place your son's coin on the ground and let me know when you've done it."

Steve did as requested and with a whoosh, Kurt was by his side.

"That's a nice trick," Steve began, "which kind of ties into your practice today."

Kurt looked around and didn't recognize the concrete columns and walkways. "Where are we?"

"Well," answered Steve, "in its more glorious days, this was the home of a major football team. But the team moved to another city, so it's our practice grounds for today."

They rounded a corner to a tunnel leading to the seating section. Master Lu was sitting in one of the seats, meditating in the afternoon sun.

"Don't mess with him. He'll be like that for hours," said Steve. "Come over here." He gestured towards a row of seats in another section. Once there, he pointed to a two-inch square metal plate which had been attached to the concrete with some type of clear adhesive. There was a pattern on the metal plate, and it was red.

"This is the starting point. It shows you a pattern for the next location which will be the next color of the visual spectrum colors going from red to violet. At each location, there will be a pattern to get you there, and the next pattern to show you where to go, but you'll mentally use the next color in rotation so you don't end up in the same place again. This will train you to spot details and memorize specifics, hopefully more quickly. I'll be at the end when you're done."

"Wait! How many are there?" Kurt asked, looking out at the stadium which could easily seat over 50,000 people.

"Well, you'll find out, but it's not like there's one on every step," Steve smirked. "Time's a ticking. Get to it."

With that, Kurt focused on the first pattern. He could get the image in his head and now he needed to change the color to orange to move to the next location. He gave Steve the thumbs up just before disappearing to the opposite side of the stadium. Steve watched him for a few turns, jumping from various parts of the stands to others on a predetermined course that he and Mr. Lu had set up days before.

Kurt decided to count the number of patterns, just in case it was going to be one of the tests Steve was going to give him later. He was in the process of memorizing the eleventh pattern when he was feeling that this was getting a little tedious if that was all there was. He focused on the pattern and suddenly found himself inside one of the rooms at the dojo. A big smile plastered his face at this surprise he wasn't expecting. He noticed a note written in masking tape stating *NEXT CLUE UNDER HERE* with an arrow pointing to a large square of concrete, easily weighing a ton—no levers, forklifts, or any other devices at his disposal to move it. Kurt concentrated and pushed on the block. It gave slowly, sliding inches at a time away from its location, finally to reveal the next metal plate underneath. Kurt memorized it and he was off again.

Detective Bailey was looking down at his watch when Kurt appeared a few rows in front of him at the beginning of the course.

"Ahh...You must've made a mistake!" laughed Steve.

"No," said Kurt, "I just wanted to say that block in the dojo was a nice addition. Now I'm off again to the next step. I hope there are more surprises." And with a whoosh, he was gone again.

Steve smiled. That kid was getting the hang of this in a way that would be very handy. He looked over his shoulder and saw Mr. Lu was oblivious to the interaction that just took place. He went back to texting Rudy and researching on his Google app while he waited for Kurt to complete his practice.

After seven more jumps within the stadium grounds, one of which landed him in a port-o-potty stall that was locked up in the parking lot, he finally had another transfer outside the stadium. This time, he appeared in a secluded wooded area, startling a medium-sized deer into a scamper. He looked around in all directions to get any kind of a bearing and couldn't place where he was. It was cold, and the trees were unfamiliar.

The next pattern was located adjacent to the one that brought him there. He memorized it and decided to look around. His dad had always told him that if he were ever stranded, to travel north and you'd eventually find civilization. He checked the trees around him, found the moss growing on the north side of the bark, and headed in that direction. He kept the pattern in mind in case he needed to make a hasty exit.

After about fifty yards through the brush and trees, he made out what looked like a cottage or cabin to the west of him. About that time, his phone started buzzing that a text was coming in. He pulled it out of his pocket.

Detective Bailey texted, *What is taking you so long?*

He texted back that he was distracted and would be finished shortly. Taking one last look at the structure, he figured he could always come back and visit again later. He concentrated on the next pattern and jumped to the next location.

Steve and Mr. Lu were waiting for him at the final spot, which was in the parking lot next to his car. Bailey asked, "So, did you like the look of the place?"

"What? How'd you know?" asked Kurt.

"Because I put the marker there, my young friend. That's my cabin in the hills of Julian. I have seven acres around that place with cameras," answered Steve. "If you went any other direction, I would have texted you earlier."

"That was fun!" said Kurt. "I hope we get to do that again."

Steve responded, "Well, if the material we used to glue those plates down stays, we'll be able to run this track again and improve on the time. Maybe we'll work on alternatives. I remember doing something similar in this very parking lot when I was a kid in Cub Scouts many years ago. We had a starting place where we'd start at a certain number along a number line, and use our compass to travel a certain number of steps in a list of directions and see which number we came back to. I think yours is a bit ramped up compared to the version I did, but I can understand the fun.

"But for now, let's go to the cabin," finished Steve.

Kurt smiled broadly, "Sure thing!"

Steve turned to Mr. Lu to tell him to watch the stuff while they were gone but, before any words came out of his mouth, Kurt touched his shoulder, and they vanished.

They arrived at the spot where Kurt had been before. After getting their bearings, they started walking to the cabin. Once they arrived, Steve pulled out his keys and opened the door. A high-pitched sound squealed until he punched in a four-digit code to the alarm box at eye level on the side wall.

"Did you get that number?" he asked.

"Yes, I saw," responded Kurt.

"Good," continued Steve. "If you ever need to get in here for any reason, you'll have the code so you can turn off the system. It'll still take video, but it won't call the cavalry. Grab a seat at the table. I'll get us a couple of sodas."

While Detective Bailey was occupied, Kurt looked around at the small but comfortable cabin. It wasn't a full-sized home by any means, but more like a studio apartment with the layout being all in the one room. The table he sat at was for two. There was a kitchen-ette, a bed, a TV, a sofa, and a wardrobe. A single person could live frugally in there, but there weren't many amenities from what he could see.

When Steve came back, he handed a soda to Kurt saying, "Looks like the refrigerator is acting up again, so it's not that cold, sorry. But I wanted to talk to you in private for a little bit."

He pulled out a small box from his pocket and put it on the table, pushing it in front of Kurt.

"Go ahead, open it up."

Kurt lifted the lid and saw several shiny intricate coins inside. He turned the box over into his hand and played with the coins between his fingers. Each one had a wing imprinted on it, and then some other symbol. They were obviously from the same set, but each was unique.

"What are these?" Kurt asked.

"These are our secret weapons. With all the pattern usage for jumping from one location to another, I thought there would be a good reason to have a select few saved aside for a special occasion," Steve answered. "Considering there may be times that we need to get in or out of tight situations, it might be a good idea to have those patterns memorized."

"Oh, I get it!" Kurt said, finally catching on. "If you put one somewhere you needed me to be, then you could text me which coin you left, and I could travel there."

"Yeah, or there are other ways to use them. But you're catch-ing on. I used the wing as your symbol to make the coins differ-ent from most other coins, and then combined with the geometric shape. They should be identifiable enough for your Stone to pick up on. Grab your phone and take photos of these so you can work to memorize them. I'll keep these with me, just so you're not tempted to toss one into a bank vault or something," Steve smirked.

Kurt started rubbing his chin, "Hey, I never thought of that..." Then he broke out in a smile, "just kidding! I have this terror of a cop always on me."

"Well," Steve began, "we had better get back. Mr. Lu is probably waiting for us to show back up. Also, your dad might be home soon, right?"

"Yup. Hold on tight." Kurt reached over and put his hand on Steve's arm, and they both vanished.

* * *

"We've only injected 12,000 people so far?!?!" Levi's voice was significantly louder than usual as he was discussing current issues during a company banquet at The Bull & Bear. There was an ample-size room they could use, but with no windows, and a controllable entrance and exit. The strict no pictures or video policy was still in effect whenever Levi was around. "Why are the numbers so low? Don't be afraid to speak."

One R&D scientist stood up and said, "I believe it's a simple case of not enough manpower."

"How did we not have enough people?" argued Levi. "If you needed more people, why didn't you just go get more to help? I mean, where were you during all this?"

"I was injecting people," he responded deadpan, which only went to infuriate Levi even more.

"Attention people. Please pay attention for a moment," announced Mendez. "It's been brought to my attention that we did not allocate enough people for injecting the population that comes to the factory. Until we can figure out how to make it foolproof for the average Joe, we can't send the machines to the stores for liability reasons.

"That being said, we need to increase the rapidity and disbursement of our product. From this day forward, if you're not in the direct line of production, or testing, or R&D, you are now an injector for the foreseeable future. I have a meeting here with some very important people, and I'm in the mood to expand. It's difficult to do that when there are 2.1 million people in this county and we've only given our product to less than one-half of one percent."

He stopped for a moment, closed his eyes and dipped his head a little. He took a deep breath and held it for a few moments before releasing it. When he spoke again, it was in a much calmer tone, but still carried as much power.

"Remember, our product is the top of the line. It's completely free to the consumer, relatively speaking. Next meeting, I don't want to have to ask where we are. I just want to hear we have a double-digit percentage of the population. Enjoy the rest of the banquet—there's about an hour left."

There wasn't much of a murmur after that. People seemed to have lost their appetite for talking, and for the food. Most left the hall in groups of three or four until the place only held Levi and one of his attorneys.

The attorney began, "You want me to help with the injections, too?"

Levi smiled for the first time that afternoon. "No, you're too expensive for that. I need you here; the senator will be here soon." He caught the attention of one of the staff members and indicated it was time to set up for his important guest.

Less than thirty minutes later, the buffet was gone, along with the large tables. Regular, private tables were reset into the dining room, with all the frills of a high-end restaurant. No patrons were escorted into this particular room, but shortly after things were in order, a couple of protective personnel entered and stood by each side of the door as the senator walked in. Both Levi and his attorney stood up immediately and walked toward him.

"Senator Strom, it's a pleasure to have you join us this afternoon," began Levi with his hand extended. "Would you please sit with us? This is my attorney and friend, Joe Ashford." Ashford shook hands in turn.

"Please, call me Jeff," the senator said as he sat down at the table. "I'm a busy man. Forgive me for being short. What exactly can I help you with today?"

Levi smiled. *You're going to help make my product a national item, something that everyone will have. No, everyone will need it!!*

Levi brought along his tablet, which had security upgrades requiring his implant. He explained this along the way while showing charts and graphs of projections and optimizations of commerce for the state, and then nationally. The senator, who was somewhat distracted at first, seemed to become very interested in the process as it unfolded. He stopped Levi several times to ask questions.

After thirty minutes, the senator's phone alarm sounded. He usually used this to make his escape from particularly boring or uncomfortable discussions. He silenced the alarm and continued to listen to what Levi was proposing. Working on the ground floor of something that could renovate the entire retail, medical, and information systems was something worth paying attention. While everyone around the two were fighting back yawns, the senator and Levi were as animated as children on a playground selecting marbles for hours.

CHAPTER SEVENTEEN

The phone rang until Steve reluctantly picked it up.

"Hello?"

"Where are you on the case?!" shouted the police chief over the phone line, causing him to pull the receiver back from his ear a few inches.

"We've gotten a few leads. We're tracking them down. We're getting a bit of push back because of the notoriety of the suspects involved," responded Steve.

"I want solutions. Did you know the mayor has personally involved himself in this? That means it's a 'must get done' case, understand?"

"I get it, sir."

Click.

Steve buried his face in his hands muttering, "Guess who that was?" to Rudy at the desk nearby.

"I could hear from here. I can imagine he was about to bust a blood vessel from the volume."

"Where are we going on this? We don't have enough to tie either of the two less likely candidates to the crime, and we certainly can't get through Mendez's lawyers to find out what he might be hiding," mused Steve. But then a thought struck him, "Rudy, Mendez spends all of his waking hours at that factory. Heck, he probably sleeps there. I bet if there're any loose ends, they might be dangling there. We've swept all three suspects' homes for DNA and found nothing, but Mendez doesn't spend much time at home."

"But what are you going to get a search warrant on? You have to have something to tie him to it and you have nothing now," countered Rudy.

"I have some phone calls to make," said Steve. Looking at his watch, *damn, make that texts to make,* noticing it was before two. He grabbed his smartphone and shot a text to Kurt asking him to call when he got out of school. He had an idea to get the information he needed, and it'd take a few days to get the process set up.

* * *

It was nearly a week later when Kurt was getting out of his computer class, after having listened about the "surprise field trip" the science department had available to Mendez MicroTech Facilities the next day. The teacher spelled out the requirements to go on the trip and passed out the permission slips. The slips also had an extra section which authorized Mendez MicroTech to inject a hardware tracker with the parents' permission, as an additional benefit to the free RFID chip insertions already going on for the public.

"I'm not a fan of shots," said Terence after school when they got together to talk about the field trip. "But, if it gives me access to all the cool stuff like they've been advertising, what's the big deal?"

"I heard someday they're going to get rid of money all together and just use this type of tech to buy and sell things," said Alan.

"I don't know," started Kurt. "You still have to get your parents' permission for that part of the trip. I just want to see all the new cool tech they have at the factory and how the robotic machines make the stuff."

"My dad will sign off—he doesn't care as long as it's free," said Alan.

"But what about those stories that the logo is showing up under the skin?" asked Terence.

"Those are just urban legends," said Alan. "They wouldn't be able to get away with that in real life. They'd get sued." And that was the icing of protection on any safety cake—the lawsuit. Case closed.

"Well, either way, we're going to see some pretty cool stuff tomorrow," Kurt added.

* * *

The next morning, the forty or so eighth graders who had their forms properly signed and dated were lining up to get on the school bus. The loud sound of the diesel engines made it hard for the kids to hear each other, so they naturally spoke louder—an event that didn't lessen the tension in the teachers' necks. Every so often, the bus would rumble and belch out a dark mass of smoke from the tailpipe. The smell of the diesel burning, the endless footsteps up and down the aisles of the bus, and the picked-at cushions at the top of each seat all spelled out public schooling. Kurt thought he could smell the metal at his feet, that tin scent and green color coated with the slip-proof rubber was enough to gag on.

The teacher made the last pass and count of each student and let the driver know it was time to go. It was two to a seat, so Kurt and Terence sat in one seat with Alan sitting across the aisle. It was fun to get away from the school for the day, but you'd think in the vast stretches of technological advances since school busses were first designed, that they would have upgraded them a little.

The factory they were going to was a thirty-minute drive from the east part of the county, so the boys just stuck their headphones in their ears and played on their phones until they arrived. The only noises were from the students who didn't charge their phones the night before and were relegated to actually view the field trip in process, making complaints along the way.

When they pulled up to the factory, they went through a security checkpoint where the guards were adorned in uniforms showing the company logo. The kids were getting excited about the new tech they were going to see shortly. Kurt checked his pockets again to make sure he had the coins that Detective Bailey had given him earlier in the week. All four were there—the fifth one was with Steve, who was anxious to hear about how this trip went. The detective had told him the backstory of what case he was working on, and why he needed access into the factory.

After check-in and a brief introduction, the guide started talking about the various aspects of the company – the year it was established, the family who started it, and some of the background. The entryway and foyer were spotless with huge monitors built into the walls advertising the many products made available by Mendez MicroTech. The foyer's high ceiling was made of glass, letting in the sun, and there were artful water fountains adorning the walls both east and west. The bubbling brook sounds made for a tranquil counterpoint to the tapping of all the sneakers of the children currently staged in the hallway.

"Wow! This place is like a palace!" said Alan to no one in particular.

He started to walk a few feet away from the group, and a man dressed in a suit with an earpiece intercepted him and urged him back to his collective.

The guide lifted her voice, "Please, everyone, stay together. This is very important. This company works on very sensitive projects and it's a privilege to allow everyone to be here today. Before we go any further, I'm sorry, but for security reasons, all phones and recording devices must be stored at the entrance to the tour."

This brought out a grumble from the kids who had their phones with them most hours of the day.

"Please, don't worry. All of your phones will be charged up and ready for you once you are finished with the tour," concluded the guide.

Reluctantly, all the phones were gathered. Kurt wondered how he was going to get information back and forth from the detective without it. He would rely on the plan they had organized and trust that it would work out. But, just in case, while everyone's attention was towards the phones being put in the case, Kurt slipped one of the coins into the cushions of the sofa in the waiting room. He knew which one it was by the feel of the mark on the surface that he'd been memorizing for days. It was decided that the coins should be placed where they wouldn't be noticed by passersby, and, hopefully, in secluded areas. There may be quite a ruckus now, but at night the lobby might be empty.

"We generally don't have tours this large, so we're going to split this into two groups," said the guide. Kurt and his friends clumped together immediately so they would be selected into the same group. "OK, here to the left will go with Sophia, and the rest will follow me.

Don't worry—everyone will get to see all the same things, just in a different order so we don't clog up the hallways."

Kurt watched Sophia walk up to direct the group of students he was in. She was tall and carried a guide paddle for the pack of kids to follow easily. While a different guide shuffled the others down the west hallway, Sophia brought Kurt's group down the east wing. She was talking about various attributes about the company's latest technologies at a backwards gait until she reached a certain point. She paused at a map of the factory premises behind a glass cabinet to show how expansive the Mendez MicroTech company was. Kurt scanned the legend quickly and made a mental note where the CEO offices were as Detective Bailey had instructed him to do.

"Now, I'm sure you've seen this in movies, but this is coming to real life for everyone to enjoy," Sophia said in a patented pseudo-enthusiastic tone. "As you can see, while I pass down the hallway here, the systems we've created are interacting with the chip I have in my hand to change the look and feel of the room to a more personalized ambiance."

As she walked, the paintings above the fountains on the walls would change to a selection more favorable to Sophia's taste. The aura-lights in the corner recesses softened their hue colors to a light green, which made her red hair stand out quite well. She made a motion with her hand and soft music started playing in the hallway to the amazement of the students—it was tantamount to magic!

Alan tapped Kurt's shoulder and whispered, "Hey, it's exactly like that movie we saw the other day with the paintings changing, but this is for real!"

"Yeah, pretty frickin' cool, isn't it?" answered back an excited Kurt. Terence was just staring in awe at the definition of the monitors. He would've sworn those were actual paintings if he didn't see them change himself.

"You'll see that Mendez MicroTech is the top of the line in all your technology needs…" Sophia continued as she came to a door with a panel to the side. "No more ID cards, or forgeries, or bad heuristics for fingerprint data. Everyone has an encrypted key code that identifies who they are and provides instant access to those areas needed." She waved her right hand over the panel and the door clicked. She pulled and ushered the rest of the group through the door to the next part of the tour.

Once they stepped past the doorway, they were led down a hall of offices to an open locker-style room.

"As you can see, Mendez MicroTech provides the safest and cleanest possible environment for both its products as well as its employees. Please take a pair of these covers and place them over your shoes like so." She demonstrated how to envelop her shoes with the covers to prevent dirty footprints in the areas they would be going. "There are several parts of the plant where employees must wear protective gear about their whole body. Please don't be afraid. There is nothing harmful that you will be near during this tour. Now, please keep close as we walk up to the catwalks."

Sophia led the students to the manufacturing building—it was state of the art. The catwalks weren't the old-fashioned walkways around a factory building like in the past, but sealed tunnels snaking through the ceiling of the manufacturing plant's outer walls, allowing visitors and workers to view the marvels of robotics going on down below on the floor. Large sheets of glass separated the group from the powerful machines, and it was thick enough to keep most of the noise at bay.

Panels of the purest white made up the walls as far as it could be seen. Robotic arms grabbing miniscule objects from tracts of assembly and piecing them together with another spot-welding arm was like watching an orchestra play. It was hypnotic to view the machines tirelessly pulling parts along and building all kinds of gadgets. The only humans in the manufacturing areas wore full contamination clothing, with computer tablets to inspect certain stages of the process.

"Look at that one," said Terence, pointing to a box where electrodes were dropped in and sparks flew out like miniature fireworks. The kids were amazed, and the guide let them soak it all in for a while.

"Who thinks up all this stuff?" was a question murmured along by several of the youths.

Sophia leaned over the slanted glass and looked down. She pointed at one of the men standing in the area below in slightly newer colored protective wear.

"Everyone, we have a surprise. If you look down there, the man in the darker blue safety gear speaking with the others is the owner of the company, Mr. Levi Mendez."

All the kids' eyes moved towards the group of employees thirty feet below watching the owner point at various components while another employee hastily made notes on his computer screen with a stylus. It was difficult to tell anyone apart from this distance, but it was obvious who was in charge by his commanding movements. Kurt looked down as the owner turned, and he felt his stomach drop as he saw red eyes and a distorted face.

He tried to compose himself as quickly as he could but asked the guide if there were restrooms available close by.

"You'll have to wait until we get down to the ground level in a few minutes, or you'll have to be escorted by one of the security personnel back to the main offices," said Sophia, not trying to hide her dissatisfaction with the interruption from her normal tour. "Is it an emergency?"

"Yes, it is," answered Kurt. He grabbed at his abdomen and walked cautiously around to emphasize the necessity to be taken to the facilities.

A few of the other kids started snickering, so the guide motioned to one of the security guards to escort Kurt back to the offices. Alan and Terence had a look of concern on their faces until Kurt winked back at them. The guard took Kurt lightly by the arm and led him back out of the corridor and down the stairs.

When they reached the restroom door, the guard waited at the doorway. Kurt entered and quickly scanned through the restroom stalls to make sure he was there by himself. He went to the largest stall and removed one of the coins from his pocket. Looking around, he finally shoved the coin behind the toilet paper dispenser wedged against the wall so no one would readily find it, and transported himself with the Stone to his bedroom.

* * *

Steve was sitting at his work desk at the precinct going through files when his phone went off. He was shocked to see it showing Kurt's home as the source call, but answered anyway.

"Detective Bailey."

"Steve, this is Kurt."

"I thought you were supposed to be on a field trip. What are you doing at home?" asked the detective.

Kurt started blurting out a bunch of things, but once Steve heard the word demon, he stopped him.

"What? Say that again?"

"The owner of MicroTech is a demon!" said Kurt. "I saw his red eyes and his face. It looked just like when I saw that guy on TV that you caught before."

"Are you absolutely sure? It wasn't a glare from the equipment or the distance that distorted your view?"

"No, I saw it for sure. I had to get back to you."

"Where do they think you are right now?" asked the detective.

"They think I'm in the bathroom having issues, so I can't stay for long. I've got to get back. But I have a problem! They are going to be injecting these things in our hands at the end of the tour and if a demon is in charge of this…"

"Then there are ulterior motives behind it," finished Steve. "Do whatever you can to avoid getting that injection. You can't let the demon know you realize what he is or you're done for."

"I get it. I'll think of something. I've got to get back soon or the guy will start looking for me. I'll meet you at Mr. Lu's after school."

Click.

* * *

Kurt focused on the coin he had just placed in the bathroom and transported back again. Upon arriving, he nearly tripped over the shoes of someone sitting on the toilet with a newspaper held up reading. His arrival caused a disturbance in the air, enough to make the occupant drop the newspaper down to look at him inquisitively.

"Oh, I'm sorry, I didn't see this stall was taken. So sorry," and Kurt as he quickly backed out of the stall. He'd have to remember to lock the stall door if he tried this application again. He exited the bathroom to an impatient guard who hurried him off to join the group again.

"What's going on?" asked Alan in hushed tones once Kurt returned to the group.

"Don't freak out," whispered Kurt. "The owner has the same color eyes as that guy we saw on TV a few weeks ago." Kurt raised an eyebrow so Terence and Alan would catch on to what he was talking about.

"No way! Really?" Terence shot back, loud enough for the guide to stop and clear her throat to get everyone's attention in the group again. The boys stood straight with smiles on their faces mimicking the apex of good behavior. The guide continued her prattle after a moment.

"Shh…We've got to figure out a way not to get stuck with that injection and hope our friends don't get stuck with it either," whispered Kurt under his breath, trying to maintain a smile while facing forward and looking attentive to the guide. "Any ideas?"

"No problem," said Alan. "It worked for me when I was going to get a flu shot I didn't want. Just wait and see."

The guide led them down the stairs to ground level and through a walkway to another building. Once they were inside, the guide started talking.

"Does anyone know what R&D stands for?"

A couple tentative hands went up. Sophia motioned to one of the students.

"Research and Demand?" answered the student sheepishly.

"Very close," Sophia said. "It's actually Research and Development. That's the area we are currently in. These are where the ideas for future technology come forth. Because of competition laws, we cannot see much of it, but we can see some of the latest tech that is about to come to market pending government approval."

A hand went up after Sophia finished her comment.

"Yes, a question?"

"Yeah, why does it require government approval?" asked one of the students.

"Excellent question. Because some technology needs to be tested by the government as safe before it can be used, or shown by trials."

She led the students around the corner to a door with notices of heavy security requirements. She opened a panel next to the door and pulled out a phone receiver. After a few words, she put it back, and the door opened.

"Wow, even she can't get in here on her own," commented Alan.

On the other side, they had to stop at a desk with a security officer. He motioned the youths through a metal detector one at a time, while watching a monitor at his desk. The lights flashed red and a signal sounded when Joey went through the scanner, but it turned out to be his belt buckle that tripped up the sensor.

"There is an absolute ban on recording instruments in the R&D area," Sophia said. "It's to protect our copyrights and keep us on the cutting edge of technology."

On the other side, they were met with a man in a lab coat.

"I am Dr. Patel, one of the research engineers here at Mendez MicroTech," he began. "I see we have a curious bunch of future scholars who would like to see some of the things we're working on."

Dr. Patel led them into a larger room lined with stations each having a different machine. It was set up as a show floor, probably for dignitaries, not for school kids. The guide ushered the kids to the first of the stations.

"OK, with a show of hands, how many of you know if your parents have gotten the RFID enhancement, yet?" asked Dr. Patel. "I mean, the chip inserted in their hand."

Only two kids in the classroom lifted their hands.

"Don't worry about that. I have one, and I'll show you how easy these devices are to operate, just like you'll be able to do once you get your chip," said the doctor as he stepped up to the first machine in the line. It was a vending machine, typically found in a school or lobby. He waved his hand in front of the pad showing the ever-present Mendez MicroTech logo. The digital display immediately lit up asking for his requested item to be selected. He pushed a couple of the buttons and a bag of chips was dispensed.

"OK, everyone, if you'll notice, each of the machines in here has a loop of plastic like this attached to a chain near the machine. If you put this device over your hand like so, it will simulate that you have a chip, and you can try the machines out yourselves."

The youths were excited when they found out about this. They weren't expecting to get to play around with some of the machinery.

"Who would like to try this out first," asked Dr. Patel.

Hands shot up all over with several kids uttering, "Pick me, pick me!"

Dr. Patel did a cursory look over the group and picked one of the girls in the front, Natalie, who stepped up to the machine and let the doctor place the loop around her fingers and slide down to sit across her palm.

"Now wave it within an inch of the surface of this logo until it registers. Good. Now, just select the item you'd like. B12, yes, go ahead and push the buttons. Excellent. Take your snack. Now remove the attachment so someone else can give it a try."

The doctor did this for one other student before moving to the next machine, another vending machine with sundry items, to perform the same task.

"So, you can see how it's going to be that much easier. On the plus side, the schools or businesses will have automatic inventory systems on what's purchased, and the parents can download everything their child uses the chip to purchase as easily as reviewing an online statement," said Dr. Patel.

At that moment, the door on the other end of the room opened, and the other guide with her group came into the room. She thought she was interrupting, but Dr. Patel waved them in.

"Your other classmates have already gotten their chips implanted, so they can start using the machines. I'll let you try out the machines for a little while and then I'll have everyone who wants to get their own chip line up at the back door where the other group came in. That's where we'll be doing the insertions."

The kids milled around a bit and talked, letting each other know that it wasn't a big deal to get the implant with the advanced machinery. Only a tiny faint red line was left where the incision was performed, and it was covered with a shiny substance that looked like a brush of clear glue. The kids who hadn't gotten the chip were starting to feel left out and meandering towards the doorway, so they'd get their own as well.

Dr. Patel walked to the door and lifted his voice, "OK, anyone who has their parents' permission for the implantation, please come this way."

Kurt was starting to get nervous. He saw Terence line up with him, but there was no sign of Alan. He quickly scanned the room with the machines and didn't see Alan's blond head anywhere. Kurt was led into the other room with the guide and the other kids.

The doctor held up a device and spoke, "This is the device we were talking about earlier. We're waiting for governmental approval to allow non-lab businesses to use them for implanting, services which have some familiarity with implanting already, but the devices do most of the work. We're talking about ear piercing kiosks, tattoo parlors, along those lines. Right now, only this office or one of our satellite offices is allowed to administer the implants with government approval."

He tilted the device so the kids could see the top of it.

"This lays on the counter, and your hand goes in here, where you'll feel it rest comfortably against a wedge. Once in place, there are scanners which map your hand. You'll feel a band stretch over your wrist to keep your hand from moving, but there is no pain involved. It takes about eight seconds once your hand is in place, and then you're finished. Who would like to go fir...."

He didn't get a chance to complete his sentence before emergency sirens started sounding throughout the room.

Dr. Patel spoke, "OK, everyone, that's a fire alarm. We need to get out of the building in an orderly fashion. Please follow me." He put the device in a cabinet, locked it, and then directed the kids back into the other room with the machine where the second half of the class was lining up. Kurt dropped a coin in the fake plant pot near the door to the room on his way out.

Surprisingly, Alan was across from Kurt in line when he looked over. Alan turned and winked at him, then put his face forward as they all started marching in semi-orderly lines to the outside, bypassing the other structures, and back to the parking lot.

The guides stayed with the kids until they were back at their bus. Sophia said to the kids, "We're really sorry some of you didn't get your implants today. We will keep your permission slips on file, and you can come back any time to get them inserted." Some of the kids were very upset they didn't get their chips that day. Within fifteen minutes, they were on the interstate heading back to school.

Chapter Eighteen

———— ◆•◆ ————

Later that day, Detective Bailey drove over to the dojo so he could catch up on what happened at the factory earlier that day. When he entered, Kurt almost stumbled over himself in excitement to tell him everything that had happened.

"Slow it down!" said Steve.

Kurt stopped himself and took a deep breath.

"OK, so we went to the factory for the field trip. They have all of the coolest technology you could imagine, but that's beside the point. When the guide pointed out the owner, I saw the exact same face as I did on that guy you arrested on TV."

"What exactly was he doing?" asked the detective.

"Well, it basically looked like he was running the company. I mean, aside from the way his face and eyes looked, there wasn't anything weird that I noticed," said Kurt. "It was almost a bummer not getting that implant that could do all the technical stuff without pushing buttons. You should have seen it! It was like magic!"

Mr. Lu came into the room at that moment with a tray carrying three mugs of steaming tea. He placed them on the table and sat with the others.

"Oftentimes, technology appears as magic to those who don't have it," said Mr. Lu after sipping a little tea.

"Well, it makes sense now that we've tracked the demon who's most likely the same one I exorcised from Finley. I'm not sure what plans he might have up his sleeve, but we've got to stop the demon before anyone else gets hurt. We've got to know what he's up to," said Steve.

He stood up and paced around for a bit to collect his thoughts.

"You put the coins where you could? Good. Between those locations and your strength, we should be able to get some type of information. If I can get close to him, I can exorcise the demon again. It won't be a solution, but it's currently inhabiting a person with potential to do damage to a lot of people," said Bailey.

"What can I do?" asked Kurt.

"You're going to help me get into that factory. If there were any other way to do it by the books, I would do it, but there isn't a judge that will give me a warrant based on my suspicions of Levi being a demon. I'm going to have to find something that I can tie back to one of the scenes of the crime and go from there, or find out what he's up to and put a stop to it."

Mr. Lu turned to Steve, "When are you planning on doing this?"

"The sooner the better, but I'm not keeping Kurt out late on a school night. We're going to have to work out a story for him. But we will need to prepare for the operation."

"I'll say I'm staying the night over at Alan's house if we do it on a weekend," Kurt offered.

"That should be good. There will probably be less employees there on the weekend as well. Today is Thursday—this weekend would be too soon to be ready, so let's shoot for next Friday night. That way, if something comes up, we could also bump it to Saturday night if we needed to."

"I'm good with that," said Kurt.

"I guess you won't need me to drive," pointed out Mr. Lu.

"Nope, not with this magic carpet," said Steve ruffling Kurt's hair.

"Hey! That's Mr. Magic Carpet to you," Kurt said laughing.

"OK. Let's meet here at nine next Friday night. I'll have all the stuff prepared, and that will give you time to talk to your dad about a sleepover coming up and get it situated."

* * *

When Kurt showed up at the dojo the next Friday evening, final classes were just getting out. He made his way to the backroom where he found Steve looking over large blueprints spread out on the table.

"Hey, glad you're here. Any problems with your cover story?"

Kurt shook his head no.

"Good. Could you look at these? I pulled them from the city planner's office, but you've been there more recently," said Steve.

Standing on the opposite side of the table, Kurt reviewed the plans laid out in front of him. He didn't know how to read them all that well, but the general shape of the building let him pinpoint the entrance and go from there.

"I put a marker here, just inside the entrance where the lobby is. I put another one over here where the office restrooms are," Kurt pointed out, "but I don't see the R&D building."

"It was a later addition," said Steve, pulling out another sheet and putting it down. "These are the pre-plans for it, but they haven't submitted the final specs."

"Yeah, it's not exactly like that," Kurt said, scratching at his temple. "That looks like the display room, which means that's the back-room with the device, so the last marker would be on the other side of a wall that would be here," he said pointing at an empty space on the sheet.

"Great! At least we have a way in for the area we need to get to," said Steve. "Are you sure you read the map correctly when you saw the CEO's offices on the second floor of the R&D building?"

"Yeah. It was there for sure," affirmed Kurt.

"Well, it makes sense from a security standpoint. That's the most guarded of all the buildings. Here, put this on," said Steve.

Kurt took off his shirt and put the bullet-proof vest on that the detective gave to him. It was bulky and itchy in all the wrong places, but safety was the key. He dug in his pocket and pulled out one of the special coins. He took some of the masking tape Steve was using to hold down the blueprints, using it to affix the coin to the under-side of the table.

"Our return ticket," said Kurt.

"Now look," the detective admonished him, "the only reason you're being allowed to go along with this is because you are a holder of a Stone and you know how to use it. But don't for a second think that means you have the option to be heroic. If anything goes side-ways tonight and you can't get near me, you zap out of there. I can fend for myself. You got it?"

"Yes, sir."

"OK, ready whenever you are," said Steve.

Kurt came around the table and put his hand on the detective's arm. With a slight inward disturbance of air and faint green glow, they were gone.

They arrived instantly next to the fake plant in the R&D's lab room where Kurt was before the fire alarm sounded. Everything looked the same as he remembered. He guided Steve over to the locked cabinet and pointed.

"That's where the new gizmo is that they're using to put the microchips in your hand," Kurt whispered.

"We knew he was going to invent newer machinery for his implants. We need to figure out what his endgame is and see if we can get in front of it," Steve whispered back.

They walked through the display room and into the front entrance area. They were able to bypass the metal detector since no one was manning the station, and walk down the corridor to the elevator and stairs to the second floor.

The elevator required a key to access, so they were relegated to the stairs. However, the door to the stairs required an electronic access pass or implant to open as well.

"Well, now what?" asked Steve, trying to find another option to get to the second floor.

Kurt thought for a second, then reached into his pocket and grabbed a coin. He memorized the face of it and flicked it under the door. A moment later and they were both on the other side of the door.

"Dang, kid, sometimes you amaze me," Steve said as they climbed the stairs to the second level.

Kurt just grinned back at him.

After entering the hallway of the second floor, they passed several doors until they reached the CEO's office. There was a small plaque next to the double doors with the Mendez logo and Levi's name and title in script. Steve listened at the door for any noises beyond. Hearing no voices, he signaled Kurt to do his door trick again.

As Kurt approached, the doors swung open to reveal Levi Mendez and three security guards standing beside him.

"Well, well, what do we have here?" began Levi. "Detective Bailey uninvited on my property and a little sidekick. Did you think I wouldn't have alarms in this building? Guards, apprehend these intruders."

"Get out of here," Steve yelled to Kurt, but Kurt stood his ground. He stood in his practiced fighting stance with his fists up.

Two of the guards went after Steve while one walked slowly to Kurt, a smile on his face.

"Whoa! Tough kid, eh? Here, I'll give you the first shot."

The guard stood towering over Kurt, putting his hands on his hips and not moving, waiting for Kurt's first shot. Kurt smirked a bit, then pulled his strength from the Stone and slammed his fist into the guard's stomach. The guard let out a pained exhale of air and flew backwards into Levi, knocking both of them to the ground.

This made the other two guards facing off Steve stop for a moment to register what just happened. It was long enough for the detective to punch one of the guards in the face and knock him to the ground. The other guard gained his composure and started battling Steve. Levi backed out of the doorway and closed the doors behind him. Shortly after, an audible alarm sounded.

Kurt was worried there would be more guards coming. He picked up the last guard by the back of his belt and slammed his head against the nearest wall, knocking him out instantly. Grabbing Steve by the arm they disappeared.

CHAPTER NINETEEN

L evi turned on his monitor. Seeing that the detective and the unknown kid had left, he turned off the alarm. Shortly after, the phone rang with the security monitoring company calling.

"No, it was a false alarm. Code word: brimstone. Thank you," said Mendez.

Levi already had ideas turning in his head. He turned to dial one of his lead computer IT employees.

"Hey, yes, I know what time it is. Get over here now. I need your assistance."

Levi kept replaying the digitized video. He couldn't believe the strength that kid had— it was unnatural. It made sense why he would be accompanying the detective, but how were they tied together? He'd have to find out who that kid was and what his relation was to Detective Bailey.

Mendez waited for over twenty minutes for the IT employee to show up. The guards had come to and apologized over and over for their inability to handle a man and a boy. Levi told them to go take care of themselves, but not mention a thing to anyone else. They were thankful for keeping their jobs and agreed they wouldn't say a word.

"What can I do to help, Mr. Mendez?" asked Chip, the IT specialist, when he finally came.

"Come over here. We had a break-in tonight."

"What? Really? Is everyone OK?"

"Don't worry about that. I need you to help me out. See this digitized video with the two burglars coming down the hallway? Is there a way to edit out the kid or edit the frame so the kid isn't in the picture?" asked Levi.

"I suppose, but why would you want to?" queried Chip.

"I'll ask the questions. You do the work. Can you do it or not?"

"Yessir. But it will take some time. Since it's a video, I'll have to do it frame by frame to do the best job. Depending on how long you want the video to be, you're looking at a minimum of twenty-nine frames per second," he responded.

Levi tapped his fingers to his chin in thought.

"I think two scenes. One in the hallway and one with the detective outside my door should be enough. Five to ten seconds of each is fine."

"No problem. That will take about five or six days unless I have help," said Chip.

"No, this is between you and me. You'll get a nice bonus in your check to keep this under wraps," said Levi.

"You got it, boss."

Levi sat back in his office chair calculating his next moves to acquire the Stone around Steve's neck while Chip began the arduous task of pixel replacement in the digital video.

* * *

Kurt and Steve arrived in a popping of air back at the dojo to the surprise of Mr. Lu who was sweeping the room.

"Whoa," he began, "you are back earlier than I expected. Did you retrieve the information you needed?"

Steve sat down at the table and buried his face in his hands.

"No. I don't think it could have gone any worse. He was ready for us by the time we got to his offices," the detective answered back. "Kurt, could you go grab some drinks for us."

When Kurt left the room, Steve asked Mr. Lu, "Would you mind using your computer to see if anything's being called in or any dispatch has been sent to the Mendez factory?"

Mr. Lu started entering Mendez MicroTech news into the Google search engine box and hit the news tab and right away different pages started showing up.

"Um… I'm not seeing anything regarding police activity, yet, but I see a couple of pages here that might be of interest from a few days ago," said Mr. Lu.

"Is there a news video feed for it? Just press that," urged Steve.

Mr. Lu accommodated him, and a window opened to display a video recording made earlier in the news.

"KISU's business brief at the top of the hour, I'm Mark Kelly filling in for Rod Anderson and this is your local business news. Stocks nearly doubled today with the announcement that Mendez MicroTech was slated to go statewide with their latest implant technology and plans to work with satellite locations throughout the rest of the U.S. to make their product available to everyone. On a side note, several credit card companies are filing suit against Mendez MicroTech for not charging any transaction fees in what they say is "unfair trade practices." So far, it's unlikely the lawsuits will gain any traction, but it is causing a problem in local markets. Some stores have stopped using the higher transactional companies in favor of the lower fees or the no-fees of Mendez MicroTech. We'll keep you informed as this story develops."

"Wow, that's a lot of product. I wonder how he's doing it all for free?" pondered Steve. "I know he makes money on his other products he sells, but this one has got to cost him quite a bit."

"Maybe he's going to wait for everyone to become dependent on it, then he'll start charging?" suggested Mr. Lu.

"That's a thought, but the government wouldn't let something like that happen. There are monopoly laws in place to prevent that sort of thing. But, whatever the reason, he's found about the only way he could make it into an established credit market going against the other carriers."

Kurt came back with hot tea for all three of them while they were talking.

"Do you think we're going to be in trouble for what we did?" asked Kurt, genuinely concerned.

Steve tried to allay the young man's fear. "I don't think so. The last thing a demon wants is a bunch of police around while he's trying to do things on the dark side, unless the police are already on the take. Plus, if he gave that tape to the police and anything happened to us as retribution, the police would know exactly where to go."

Sipping his tea, he closed his eyes for a moment hoping what he told the kid was the truth. Then he continued, "He knows who I am. He also knows that I'm after him for more than just a murder case. I know what he is. What we need to do is figure out how we're going to put an end to him. I've never had a demon continue to come back at me over and over again. I need to exorcise him permanently."

"How are you going to do that?" asked Kurt.

"I have no idea. My ability has only been able to pull the demon out of the host like a virus," answered Steve. "The demon will just hop into another body unless I figure out a way to deal with him."

"What if we dropped one of my coins in the ocean, then I transport him there and transport back really quick?" suggested Kurt.

"I like your bravery, but you'd be crushed instantly, and the demon would just float to the top and escape. Demons don't need air. You'd just be killing the host," said Steve.

He ruffled Kurt's hair and said reassuringly, "We'll figure something out. But for now, it's time for home. Get back to a normal routine and put this debacle behind us." He hoped he sounded somewhat convincing. "I have to get back to the evidence and see if I can tie Mr. Mendez to any of the crimes legitimately. Now we know for a fact he's the one that did it, maybe there's something Rudy and I can pick up on. A demon wouldn't stay inside a prisoner for long. Right now, he's protected, and it'll be harder and harder to get to him as he becomes more powerful. But if we can get him caged, there's nothing he can do."

The detective stood up and grabbed his keys from the table.

"C'mon, I'll give you a ride back to your complex."

CHAPTER TWENTY

T here was a knock at the office door. Levi yelled for whoever it was to come in.

"Chip, good to see you. Come on in. Let's talk," he said.

Chip took a confident step into his boss' office, closed the door, and, with a smile on his face, brandished a USB thumb drive in his hand.

"Guess what I have?"

"Really? A day early? Yes, yes, please show me," said Levi.

Chip put the drive in the owner's computer and pulled up the footage he had been working on for the past five days. It was a clear eight seconds of Detective Bailey walking down the hallway towards the CEO's office, and another six seconds of him listening at the door. There was no sign of the kid in any of the video footage.

"That's perfect, thank you! And the still shot of the kid?" asked Levi.

"Sure thing. It's a separate graphic file on the USB. Here it is. I'll print it to your printer," said Chip.

At that time, another knock came at the door. It was Beverly from accounting.

"I have payables requiring your signatures, Mr. Mendez," she said.

"OK, grab that paper off the printer and bring everything over here," Levi responded.

She did so and brought the checks to have her employer sign.

"What's this? A check to the fire department for $1,250? What's that for?" asked Levi.

"That's for our third false alarm to the fire department the other day when the kids were visiting the plant. We didn't have our permit posted in the correct location and it wasn't updated, so we were hit with the fine. Do you want me to try and see if insurance will cover it?" asked Beverly.

"Oh, that's right. Yes, please check and see. Here's the rest of the checks, you can get back to your work."

She took the rest of the checks and left the room, closing the door behind her.

"I had forgotten about those kids coming here a couple of weeks ago for the tour. Maybe our little burglar could be one of them. I'm going to need your skills again, Chip. Can you sort through the video feeds from that time frame and see if you can pick up any kid that looks like this picture? That would help me quite a bit."

"Sure thing, boss. You know you could just give the information to the police and they could do the same thing," Chip offered.

"I prefer to handle things myself," Levi responded.

Chip was smart enough not to ask anything further.

"I'll leave you to this. Work here so no one will disturb you. I have to meet up with the Senator for a press conference this afternoon."

"You got it, boss."

Levi spent a few minutes getting ready in the office before calling his driver to take him to the conference. Since the detective had seen him, there was no point in hiding from cameras or videos any longer. As long as the detective had that Stone around his neck, Levi had to stay away from him, and he could do that with legality, bodyguards, and a plan he was working on.

After entering the car, Levi had the driver pick up his attorney, Joe Ashford, to explain his ideas on the way.

"You handle that part while I'm at this conference," said Levi. "I'm making the announcement with the Senator about his bill which will mandate all U.S. military forces to have the chip implanted for identification purposes. It's to replace the military dog tags. Hopefully, it'll pass through Congress quickly, and we can see our results starting in a couple of weeks."

"Brilliant idea, Mr. Mendez," responded Joe. "Mandating something that hundreds of thousands have to use will start making it the norm rather than the exception. Our contracts with the online streaming services are rock solid. We're even starting to get requests from the credit companies to allow services to be bound to your chip."

Levi smirked and said, "Let them squirm for a while, the way they make all of their customers squirm. We'll eventually allow them, but it'll be on our terms, not theirs."

"Very well," said Joe. "Any other last-minute instructions?"

"Just make sure you don't leave the file with the police. That's our property," said Levi.

"Will do."

The car slowed to a stop and the attorney walked confidently into the precinct, not looking back.

* * *

Steve was going through evidence files for the third or fourth time, trying to find something he may have missed. Rudy, sitting opposite of him, was doing the same thing after being informed that Levi should be their top priority.

The phone rang at his desk. After speaking for a moment, he put the phone down.

"That was the chief. He wants to see me in his office," said Steve.

"Does he want the both of us?" asked Rudy, not relishing the idea of a beating down for not producing results.

"No, just me. Keep working. I'll be back."

Steve walked down the hall and upstairs to the chief's office. He knocked on the door and was told to come in. He walked in to see the chief at his desk with another man sitting to the side with a laptop open in front of him, sharing the screen with the chief. Steve instantly didn't trust the guy by the level of self-importance he carried. Aside from the Armani suit he was in and the tightly clipped goatee he wore that looked like every hair was measured individually, he just reeked of attorney.

"This is Joseph Ashford," started the chief, "the attorney representing the business and personal interests of Levi Mendez."

There was no attempt from either party to entertain handshakes, so the chief continued.

"Mr. Ashford has some interesting video documentation which he just showed to me which I find quite interesting. Mr. Ashford, would you please replay that for Detective Bailey?"

The attorney turned the laptop around on the chief's desk and restarted the video. It clearly showed Detective Bailey walking down the hallway of the factory office building. There was no denying who it was. Oddly, he didn't see Kurt anywhere in the video. He couldn't remember if Kurt was behind him or off to the side in that particular hallway, but he wasn't there. He saw enough and looked downward. Mr. Ashford stopped the video and closed the laptop.

"Mr. Ashford, thank you for your time. Please let your employer know that things will be handled appropriately," said the chief standing up. He shook hands with the attorney and led him to the door and closed it. He waited for quite some time at the door before turning around to return to his desk.

He sat down, leaned back in his chair, and folded his hands in front of his chin, creating a steeple with his index fingers across his mouth while his elbows rested on the chair's armrests. The only giveaway was the throbbing artery in his neck showing the level of tension he was feeling about the situation. Steve was smart. He kept his mouth shut and didn't bother to give excuses.

With a voice almost more fearful for its calmness, the chief began, "Do you have any idea what you might have done? Of all the idiotic ideas I've heard in the twenty-seven years I've been here, there's not one that's going to make me believe you had a good one for breaking into a suspect's business without a warrant."

The chief's voice was steadily gaining volume, ever so slightly.

"Do you realize that if you had found anything, ANYTHING at all, it would have been tainted evidence and it could have compromised the entire investigation?"

The chief's face was palpably turning pink by this point, and then a beeping sound started sounding from his wrist. He paused, breathed a few times. The beeping stopped.

"You've been a dependable officer and detective for a long time. Luckily, the guy isn't pressing charges— BUT HE COULD IF HE WANTED TO!" His wrist started beeping again. He stopped and removed the wristband, tossing it in his top drawer.

"I have no choice but to take you off this case."

Steve reacted to this, "But, chief…"

"No, no buts! Give everything you have to Rudy. Your hands are off of it. It's the only chance this case has of not being tossed. I'm also collecting your gun and badge. You're on suspension without pay for the next thirty days."

Steve's heart dropped in his chest. He'd never been in this much trouble before. He pulled his badge off his belt and the holster from his side, and placed them on the chief's desk.

"Look, Bailey, take this time to think about things. We have to follow the rules so we don't become like those we're after. You start cutting corners and you bring us all down. Don't take the law into your own hands and start rewriting the way things are. Spend this time getting your head straight."

Steve nodded and turned around. He had nothing to say. He couldn't tell the chief why he did what he did or give any excuses because the chief wasn't a party to the war that he was in. A war that went beyond case law and textbooks, judgements and paroles, to the very heart of good versus bad.

As he reached the door, he turned and said to the chief, "Sir, I'm sorry for my actions, but I want you to know that from the bottom of my heart, I know Mr. Mendez is the murderer we're after. I just wanted to bring something evil down, but I understand the rules and why they're there."

He walked out of the office and went to his car and sat in it. He'd give Rudy a call later, but for now, he just needed to drive for a while.

CHAPTER TWENTY-ONE

———◦•◦———

It was early on a school morning when Kurt was leaving his apartment. He had his jacket on with the hood pulled around his face to keep himself warm. While he was backing out the door to his private patio about to lock it, a strong arm snaked around his waist. A bulky hand covered his mouth quickly, and he felt a painful injection in his neck. In seconds, he was woozy, and everything faded to black.

The two henchmen picked up Kurt's body and carried him back into the house. Looking around quickly, they noticed an area rug in the living room. They pulled the coffee table off of it and rolled up Kurt. Then, carrying their capture over their shoulders, they walked out briskly and placed him in the van they had in the back parking lot. Driving off, unnoticed, it was a three-minute job start to finish. Mr. Mendez would be happy.

While one was driving, the passenger picked up his cell phone.

195

"Yes, Mr. Mendez. We have the package…No, there were no problems at all…OK, we'll arrive at the marina in just over half an hour…Yes, sir, I know, the boy will not be harmed in any way. He's just sleeping pretty right now."

The driver looked in his rear-view mirror, then over to his partner.

"You better get started. The boss said to make sure he stays under no matter what."

"I know," said the other henchman, getting up. He crouched and half-walked to the back of the truck to unwrap the rug and place Kurt on a gurney that was on one side of the van. A stainless-steel rod was near one end with an I.V. bag and tube hanging from it. While he prepped Kurt for the insertion, he looked at the road ahead.

"Try to make it as stable as you can for a few seconds, eh?"

Luck was on his side, puncturing the vein on the first try and taping down the needle so the solution would keep Kurt in stasis. He figured the kid was supposed to be kept asleep so he couldn't identify anyone, or something like that. He just did as he was told and was paid well for it. He patted Kurt down and found his cell phone, removing the battery and placing both parts in a plastic bag. After making sure everything was in order, he returned to the front seat to wait out the trip to the marina for the rest of the job.

Thirty minutes later, they were backing the van into the loading area. After opening the back door, a drape was placed over Kurt and the IV rod was lowered so it could have been anything being moved down the dock to the boat. The henchmen were able to handle the weight and made it look easy carrying the gurney through awkward portions until it was safely inside the yacht.

Levi came with the photo print to verify it was the same boy. Looking at the two images side by side, he smiled. He had the henchmen lock the gurney to the cabinetry where there was a glass refrigerator showing several more IV bags available for future use. One of the henchmen handed Levi the baggie with the phone. Levi pulled Kurt's collar down expecting to see a necklace with a Stone, but he didn't see one. He checked Kurt's wrists for a bracelet or something and found nothing.

"Did either of you notice a necklace or bracelet?" asked Levi.

"No, sir. Just the phone."

Turning back to Kurt, Levi said, "You are quite the mystery, my little friend, but you are going to bring me what I've been waiting a long time to get my hands on."

To the others he charged, "Keep an eye on him. I have a few things to handle, but I'll be back. Make sure he stays asleep. He's quite the danger when he's awake."

The others didn't look convinced, but they wouldn't go against him.

* * *

Mr. Lu was at the gas station down the street from his martial arts studio. He used his credit card for pay-at-the-pump as always, but it said there was an error. He tried another card with the same result. Looking into his wallet and only seeing a five-dollar bill, he walked into the store to see if he could get it filled from the attendant.

"Hi. I'm trying to use the pump, but my cards aren't working on number four."

The attendant smiled and said, "We've been having problems with the readers all morning. Let me try it here."

He took Mr. Lu's card and tried several times, with no luck.

"Do you have a chip or cash?" asked the attendant.

"What?"

"Do you have the chip implant? Those are working fine right now. Or, I can take cash, but the other credit cards are not working now," said the employee.

"Here's five dollars on pump four. I don't have a chip," responded Mr. Lu.

He returned to his car and pumped his gas, noticing several police cars flying past the gas station with their lights on and sirens blaring.

Driving back to the dojo, he locked himself in and turned on the news. Before he could get settled, the phone rang.

"Mr. Lu, this is Jim Palmer, Kurt's dad. I got a phone call from the school this morning that he didn't show up for some of his classes. I was hoping you might have seen him. I've tried calling his phone, but it goes straight to voicemail. I've tried calling the police, but the phone lines are jammed. I'm really worried."

"Mr. Palmer, I have just arrived at the studio and there is no sign of Kurt. I will make some phone calls to those I know he hangs out with from here, and I will let you know if I hear anything," assured Mr. Lu.

"Thank you so much. Goodbye."

Click.

Mr. Lu didn't hesitate in calling Detective Bailey.

"Hello?"

"Steve, this is Mr. Lu. Kurt is missing."

"What?"

"His dad just called, and he didn't make it to school. When he calls, it goes to voicemail. Can you find out where his phone is?" asked Mr. Lu.

"I'd have to call in a favor or two. I'm currently suspended. Tell you what, I'll get down there shortly, and we'll figure this out."

"OK."

Click.

It was less than twenty minutes before Steve was at the dojo standing with Mr. Lu.

"I tried calling the main line on my way here and something's wrong, but I was able to get through to one of my friend's cell phones. She's trying to triangulate Kurt's last location and she'll call me back."

Two El Cajon police cruisers raced north on second street with their sirens blaring.

"Pull up some news to see what's going on," suggested Steve.

Mr. Lu turned on the TV in the waiting room of the studio and fiddled with the controller until he landed on the local news station.

"...Sid Price of KFNT again, our earlier story has continued to dominate the news as we receive more and more reports of locations where small standoffs are happening all over the county due to issues with payment systems. Earlier this morning, it appears someone had activated a virus in the software of the systems which use transactional software for point of sale. That's right. All major credit and debit cards are not functioning at point of purchase. We're keeping you updated on what's going on. It seems retailers are accepting cash and the chip implant is working since it's a newer system installed. More to come as the situation develops..."

Mr. Lu turned to Steve, "Should we have gotten those implants after all?"

"No," Steve answered back. "If it's the design of the demon, there can't be anything good in it for us, no matter how easy it looks."

Steve's friend was taking a long time, so he tried calling her again.

"Yes, I understand, but this is important. OK, just let me know when you know something," he said.

Steve put his phone back in his pocket. "Their resources are spread thin. She can't give me any time to work on my missing persons while all the other chaos is going on.

"Steve, look at this," said Mr. Lu pointing to the TV screen.

Detective Bailey could barely contain himself when he saw Levi Mendez talking to the news teams in an impromptu session outside his factory.

"…everyone, yes everyone can get their implants for free. Just go to our website to find your local locations to have it done and you can process all your transactions without an issue. I abhor the idea of people fighting and rioting. This does not have to be the case. Please, get the implant and everyone can enjoy the benefits it provides…"

The scene cut back to the anchors, "This is Sid Price still at the desk while this economic catastrophe is going on. Personally, I'm thankful I already got my implant." He held up his right hand to the camera. He covered his ear and bent his head to the side for a moment. "This just in, banks are closing their doors from the rapid withdrawal of cash from accounts. Many stores are only accepting cash or MicroTech chips. Please, if you don't have a reason to go outside, stay home while this crisis is going on."

"Dammit," said Steve, "that's the demon's doing. This was the long con, to get everyone to get those implants so all of the economy would somehow go through his business."

"What does a demon care about money?" asked Mr. Lu.

"Because money is power, and demons crave power in all its forms," answered Steve. "He's got everyone by the wallet."

There was a knock at the glass door. It was hours before any students were supposed to arrive. Mr. Lu answered the door to a visibly devastated Jim Palmer.

"I'm sorry for imposing, but I know my son spent a lot of time here. I tried calling, but all the phone lines are down now. I just want to find my son," said Jim. "Did you hear anything about him? With all these things going on, the police won't help."

Steve walked up to Jim and introduced himself.

"Mr. Palmer, I am Detective Steve Bailey. Please sit down here. Perhaps I should have made myself known to you a while ago, but..."

Steve's phone rang, piercing the tension. "Hey, it's Kurt! Hold on. Let me get this."

"Hello?"

"Sorry to disappoint, detective," came the raspy voice on the receiver, "but Kurt isn't available to play now." Steve instantly recognized the demon's voice. "He's sleeping nicely like another little boy I used to know."

"You better not hurt one hair on him," said Steve. He pulled the phone away from his ear and put the phone on speaker.

"Oh? Not like when I pinched the mouth and nose closed of a certain little boy because I was sick of his screams?" came the guttural voice from the speaker. Mr. Palmer looked panicked and Mr. Lu put a hand on his shoulder to steady him.

"What do you want, demon?" asked Steve, visibly agitated.

"Same thing I've always wanted. Come to the Shelter Island Marina, slip 616, by yourself, and we'll make a trade. If I see anybody else there or any police, the boy is done and I'm sailing away. You have one chance to get this right. I'll be there in two hours. You know I hate to leave things living..."

The phone went dead.

"What's going on?" asked Jim. "I mean, what's really going on?"

Steve took a deep breath, and then began explaining about the Stones, the Archangels, demons, and the most recent developments with Mendez MicroTech.

201

Jim looked down, nodded his head a couple of times, then laid a hook across Steve's face. Steve wasn't ready for it and bowled over.

"I don't know what kind of bullshit you're trying to pull on me, but I want to know where my son is," cried Jim as he jumped on top of Steve, pounding his fist into his face over and over.

Mr. Lu reacted quickly to pull Jim back and off.

"No, I deserve it," said Steve, getting up, blood running down a cut near his eye and his nose. "I put Kurt in danger, and I should have looked out better for him." He reached up and wiped at his eye and nose, and the cut was gone, along with the blood, like it never happened.

"What the…" Jim started.

"I was telling you the truth," said Steve. "These Stones are real, and your son is a holder of one of them. And your wife? She had the genes to hold a Stone and she was sensitive enough to see the demons without a Stone— it drove her mad, and no one would believe her."

Jim buckled, fell to his knees sobbing. He felt he had lost everything, like the world was turning upside down. Kurt was his anchor in the storms of emotion he felt over the years of losing his wife.

He composed himself, and said under his breath to Steve, "You will go bring back my son. You owe me that much. Do whatever it takes but bring him back."

Steve didn't wait a moment longer. He walked out the door and drove off.

CHAPTER TWENTY-TWO

W hile driving by the local shops near his house, Steve noticed several stores with handwritten signs displaying "MicroTech Chip or Cash Only," most abbreviating Microtech to the logo "111." Some of the locations with hired help were checking to make sure people had implants or cash before letting them in the stores. They would have to flex their fist to let the MicroTech logo show through their skin.

What is this world coming to? Steve thought to himself. He pulled into his house and changed into his jeans and leather jacket to ride his motorcycle. He figured the further downtown he went, the more chaotic it might be, so a motorcycle would be easier to navigate. He locked his son's helmet into the holder on the side of the bike for Kurt, if needed.

While kneeling on the ground, he said a prayer asking for help in what was about to happen. He knew lives were on the line, and he didn't want to make the wrong decisions, but he couldn't shake the image of Mr. Palmer telling him to bring his son back. He hopped on the motorcycle and started off towards the highway.

Steve followed the eight-freeway west until he exited by the San Diego Bay, turning south to reach Embarcadero Marina. He knew where it was from the concerts he had gone to at a local venue nearby.

He pulled up to the entrance of the marina and parked. A lot of activity was going on the docks. Deckhands and captains were taking dollies of canned goods onto their boats, along with containers of water. There was a sense of urgency in their walk. Steve left his helmet locked on his bike and started walking along the docks to find the yacht where the demon was holding Kurt captive. The sun was starting to dip into the western sky, making the shimmering off the ocean straight ahead hard to see.

As he approached slip 616, he heard a raspy voice tell him, "Welcome, Detective Bailey. Please come aboard." The yacht was easily 150 feet long, with a surplus of amenities that Steve would have found fascinating on another day. At this moment, he was walking the deck towards the stern where he heard the voice come from, and preparing himself for anything.

Turning the corner, Steve saw Levi with a gun to Kurt's temple on a gurney. Kurt wasn't moving at all. There were two thugs nearby.

"Again, welcome Detective Bailey. No need to be agitated. We are all civilized people here," said Levi, the guttural voice merged with the slick salesman type voice of the host.

"Would you like to shake hands?" Steve offered.

"Oh, very funny. You know with all those germs going around, let's just keep our hands to ourselves, OK?"

Steve took account of the surroundings. If he could get in contact with Levi, he would be able to exorcise the demon and get Kurt free. But while Kurt was incapacitated, he was a liability. He slept soundly, the same way his son, Christopher, used to sleep. The image was racking his emotions along with Mr. Palmer's demands.

"It seems you have all the power. What do you need me for?" asked Steve.

"Power!" Levi smiled, "you have no idea what true power is. True power is to hold others' lives in your grasp, to snuff it away on a whim."

Levi pulled the gun up and shot the two henchmen in the back of the head. They had no idea what was coming. Steve stared wide-eyed at the lack of compassion or empathy.

"See? That is true power. But it wouldn't do me any good to shoot you would it, Mr. Bailey?"

Steve tried to collect his thoughts. He knew demons were evil and detested life, but he didn't know how little this demon cared for it. He might actually shoot Kurt if he didn't get his way.

"No, we seem to be at somewhat of a stalemate, Mr. Mendez," Steve said. "On one hand, you can't take my Stone, and you can't kill me. On the other hand, I can't kill you, I would just be killing your host body." Steve took a step closer.

"Ah, ah, ah…" said Levi, returning the gun to Kurt's temple. Steve stood still.

"Chess it is, Mr. Bailey, and you wouldn't want me to sacrifice your pawn, would you?"

"Let's be real. How do I know you wouldn't kill either of us if I gave you the Stone anyway? You'd have all the cards."

"Mr. Bailey," Levi began, "I will have that Stone if I have to line up a million innocent people to die."

"What are you talking about?"

"I didn't think you'd give up your Stone for just one person, no matter how much he reminds you of your boy. But, if you don't give me that Stone, I will set in motion my little insurance policy. In each of the implants is a small biotoxin that can kill its host in a matter of hours. It makes Ebola look like the common cold. I know you probably could handle one life on your conscience, but can you handle one million lives?"

"You bastard!" Steve was rocked back. He took a few breaths with his head down and eyes closed. "Fine. You'll leave us alone, and everyone will live?"

"Yes, I believe everyone with an implant should live if I get my goal," said Levi.

Steve reached around his neck and took off his Stone. He never thought this day would come. He felt dirty and wrong, but he bundled up the chain and rock in his hand and tossed it halfway towards the gurney where Levi was.

"That was kind of a wimpy throw," said Levi.

"I can't exorcise you now. I want to check and see if Kurt is OK."

"As you wish."

Levi started walking towards the chain and Stone. Steve worked his way around Levi with his hands in the air to get to Kurt's side to see how he was.

Once Levi reached the chain, he put the gun down and put the necklace over his head. The Stone lay against his shirt but started burning a hole to his chest. The light from the Stone started getting brighter. Levi screamed in pain. He tried to rip the Stone off, but it was embedded into his skin and bones, burning brighter.

Steve took the opportunity to pull the gun from his ankle holster and fired to center mass. Levi was rocked back. He looked down, seeing blood seeping from the bullet hole, not comprehending what was going on through all the pain. Steve fired again, hitting Levi's shoulder, spinning him back to the edge of the deck. Steve kept firing and Levi eventually dropped overboard into the ocean leaving a streak of blood as a mark where he was.

Bailey pulled the needle out of Kurt's arm and found a first aid kit. Using the smelling salts, he was able to revive Kurt, but he was still groggy. The detective noticed the necklace wasn't in place and asked Kurt about it.

"Oh, I put it in my jeans extra pocket wrapped in toilet paper when I go to school, so it doesn't look noticeable and I don't have the chance of doing something like I did with Mackey again."

Steve wiped his face with his hand and said, "Well, put it on and get some of your strength back. You've been out of it all day. Your dad is worried sick about you. Oh, by the way, I had to fill him in on all the details."

"Whoa, how'd he take it?" asked Kurt.

"With a right cross against my face," Steve said. "We'll talk about it later. Let's get out of here."

They started walking up the pier and heard a bubbling sound coming from the water. Looking back, the yachts in the marina were starting to sway to port and starboard. They were almost to the gate, and the entire pier seemed to be undulating.

"This can't be good," said Steve.

Out of the water a horn poked, followed by three other horns, attached to the head of a serpent-like creature. The front horn had the stone of Raphael embedded into it. Looking out across the water, several more spiky horns started to show, singularly, each with a serpent head, seven in all. Each head was attached to a sinuous long neck, nearly pitch black in color. One of the heads had what looked like a scar on it. It was three slash marks with hooks at the top.

"Does that look like the MicroTech logo to you?" asked Kurt.

"Oh my God. Kurt, get on. We need to go," Steve said with urgency.

They got on the motorcycle as the beast was inching its way towards the coast, finally pulling a limb out of the ocean and bringing the rest of its body in tow. It was massive, over a city block long, and easily 300 feet tall. The heads were darting around on the serpentine necks, all connected at the base of a cat-like body. Boats were swept aside with the massive tail as it started to walk.

Kurt looked back to make sure they were getting away from the creature and saw formidable destruction from the nameless beast. When they were able to put a good distance between them, Steve stopped the motorcycle and took off his helmet. It was so surreal he couldn't process everything at once.

Kurt asked, "What happened? Why does it have that marking? Is that Levi Mendez?"

Steve kept his eyes on the destruction in the distance. "No, that's not Levi Mendez any longer."

He pounded the thumb side of his fist to his forehead, "How could I have been so stupid? How could I have missed the signs?"

"What signs?" asked Kurt.

"That logo you call MicroTech isn't what it appears to be. I didn't remember from my schooling when I was younger, but the Hebrew number six looks like one to us. That logo isn't a 'M,' it's three sixes," said Steve. "And that means we're in a lot more trouble than I thought we were."

"We've got to warn people to evacuate!" cried Kurt.

Steve looked east and saw a few helicopters coming in, smaller than the military.

"Those are news helicopters. Let's see if we can find out what's going on."

They sped away to an electronics big box store in the southeast of downtown San Diego. Windows were already smashed out, and several people were looting the place, pulling all types of technical gear out of the store. Steve and Kurt walked in, barely hindered, to see the TV displays highest on the walls that weren't touched. The sound was out, but the closed captioning was letting them know what was going on in the images.

"… [large unknown type of beast ravaging the downtown area of San Diego.] [I haven't seen anything like this before.] [*Beast spews gaseous red cloud from one mouth*] [See that? It's turning some people into melting piles of mush, but others are completely unharmed!] [The unhurt ones are cheering for the beast all along G Street?!]"

The scene showed another of the serpent heads smash into a building, belching out a liquid, which ate away at the structure, large blocks of misshapen concrete dropping to the street below. It pulled its head back out, and the building fell. Rows and rows of what appeared to be homeless people in the downtown area were cheering the beast on, unaffected by anything the beast spat out. Just then, military helicopters came into view and the news helicopters soared back to give way. Several missiles from the military choppers flew at the creature, but nothing happened. One head whipped out and crunched down on a flyer that got too close. Others were whisked around by the tail of the creature.

As time went on and Kurt and Steve watched in shock, jets from the nearby bases were finally sent in, lobbing their missiles, but to no effect. They watched as even the most powerful bombs would create a small perforation in the scales of the beast, but then heal over in seconds. The Stone on the head with four horns glowed a dull blood red, matching the color of the creature's multiple eyes.

"Without my Stone, I can't do anything," said Steve. "I can't believe I let this happen."

"You didn't have a choice! He was going to kill millions if you didn't," said Kurt.

"I don't know that for a fact. What I do know for a fact is we're screwed! It looks like the only people immune to the beast are those who have implants. I saw somewhere that the homeless were the first to sign up for the implants hoping to take advantage of the free giveaways that came with it," argued Steve.

"Wait, I just thought of a plan," said Kurt.

"No, you're not going to drop this thing at the bottom of the ocean. You're not giving your life up for this. It probably wouldn't do anything to the beast anyway," pressed Steve.

"No, something else. Do you still have your son's coin with you?" asked Kurt.

"Yes, I always carry it with me. Here."

Kurt looked at it for a moment, remembering the nuances of the coin.

"OK, I need you to get this coin somewhere close to the heads of that beast, at least close enough to yell at it," said Kurt. "Can you do that in say, fifteen minutes?"

"Sure, but what are you thinking…" He didn't get time to finish the sentence when Kurt popped out of the scene.

Steve didn't wait, he turned and ran out to the parking lot. A looter was trying to steal his motorcycle, but he knocked the guy off with a punch to his face and got on. He didn't bother putting on his helmet when he started the motor up and peeled out of the parking lot, the front tire slightly lifting from the ground.

He zipped through the streets, avoiding crowds of people panicking, keeping parallel with the creature. He looked to his left and saw the clawed foot step down, only a couple of blocks away, and then heads snaking around the buildings. There was only one way to be sure the beast would be near a building, and that was to get out in front of it.

Steve punched it again, weaving around the traffic, sometimes taking the sidewalks when the cars were too congested. A few blocks ahead he saw something to grab his interest. A partially renovated building with a large crane attached several blocks away. It had scaffolding and a construction elevator. Most likely, no one would be in the building for whatever Kurt had in mind. He sped off in that direction hoping he'd have enough time to get to the right floor.

* * *

Kurt popped into his bedroom and startled his dad who was sitting on his bed.

"Kurt, what…?" started Mr. Palmer.

"Hi, Dad. Detective Bailey told you about the Stones, right?" asked Kurt.

"Yes, but he didn't go into detail. I'm just so glad you're OK. You are OK, aren't you? I was at the martial arts studio looking for you, but there were so many rioters in the streets, I came back home to wait to see if you'd be back."

"Yes, Dad, I'm fine," said Kurt and gave his dad a hug. "But I don't have a lot of time. I need to get back to help out Steve."

"What's going on?" asked his dad.

"Really? You haven't seen it yet?" Kurt flipped through his phone to YouTube to find a news piece about what was going on downtown and tossed it to his dad. His dad's face paled as he watched what was happening.

"That's really happening here? Now?"

"Yes, and I've got to go help," said Kurt.

"You're doing no such thing!" said Mr. Palmer. "I just got you back. You're not going into danger again."

"Dad, trust me on this one. Everything happens for a reason. I may be the only one who can help stop this thing." Kurt stuffed a few more items in his pockets, threw on a different jacket, and was ready to go.

"Wait!" his dad stopped him. "You're all I have. Wherever you go, I go. Can you take me with you?"

They locked eyes. Kurt didn't need to ask if his dad was sure. He put his hand on his dad's shoulder, checked the time on his phone, and they popped out of the room.

* * *

The elevator shook every time the beast took a step. Steve held on to the hand rails as he ascended the outside of the building. He could see the Beast coming only a few blocks away, with a wake of destruction behind it. The seven heads with their menacing horns would breathe out various contaminants smelling of disease and rot. Still, hundreds of people followed behind, unaffected by the vitriol, rooting for the beast to plow down the buildings of the rich and powerful.

Steve stopped when he was about eye level with the creature's heads. Exiting the elevator, he placed the token on the ground, stepped back and waited. He had a couple of minutes remaining, but he hoped Kurt would be sooner rather than later. He took the time to say another prayer, feeling relief at how much it relaxed him in this horribly tense situation. The beast was approaching closer, the glowing red eyes seemingly staring directly at him, mocking his choice to give away his Stone.

Just then, Kurt and his dad appeared nearby. Steve was a bit shocked to see the added arrival and put his hands up to signify he didn't want to fight.

Jim said, "Don't worry about it, my son is back. Holy..." He looked out the window and saw the beast for the first time coming directly towards them. "Why are we here again? We should be getting the hell out of here!"

Kurt ran to a nearby desk. "Steve, help me break out one of the windows."

Steve got behind the desk and pushed as hard as he could. The desk skidded along until it smashed one of the large office windows and the desk fell out to the street below. It made enough noise to attract the attention of the beast, gaining the main head's interest.

Kurt started taking his necklace off and removing the stone from the chain.

Steve looked at him oddly and asked, "What are you doing?"

Kurt reached into his back pocket. He said, "There's something I forgot to tell you..." Pulling out his slingshot and manning it on his left arm, he slid the Stone of Gabriel into the leather pocket with his right hand and pulled back as hard as he could. "...my Stone doesn't like snakes."

"What..." was all Steve got out when Kurt launched the Stone. In midair, it started to grow and glow green. First the size of a walnut, then a softball, then a basketball – by the time it got near the beast, it was larger than the main head. The green fireball connected, and the head was engulfed with supernatural flame. Sizzling and popping sounded, and then smaller fireballs darted out to encompass the other heads of the beast. The screaming emitting from the mouths of the beast pierced the air, hurting their ears. Until finally, the fire burned out and the necks dropped to the ground, letting out hot black ichor which looked like tar. The body seemed to be dissolving into that substance as it gained viscosity.

Steve ran and hugged Kurt, then put him down and passed him to a grateful Jim.

"Wait, how'd you know that would work?" asked Steve.

"I didn't. Remember when I was trying to tell you about using the Stone in a slingshot? One of the things I did was take out a diamondback from thirty yards away," said Kurt.

"Wait, you equated that thing to a snake?" asked Steve.

"Hey, it was snake-ish. Besides, I didn't have any other ideas," grinned Kurt.

"Well, let's get down there. It might take us a while to find our Stones in that muck. But I don't want anyone else to get hurt touching them," suggested Steve.

The three men got into the elevator and closed the doors.

"No, I get to work the controls."

"Why? Let me!" ...and then the elevator was moving.

Chapter Twenty-THREE

A few days later, Steve was in the chief's office, resignation letter in hand.

"You know, son, everyone makes mistakes. It's a suspension. It doesn't mean you have to quit."

"I know," said Steve. "But lately I've been figuring things out for myself and I think I have a different calling than I did before."

"Well, if you ever change your mind…"

Steve stood up and stuck out his hand. The chief did the same, exposing the alert band that was beeping last time he was in this office.

Steve focused for a moment and said, "Thank you, sir. You're not going to need that alarm band any longer."

Breaking the handshake, the chief smiled sarcastically, "Yeah, like you're the only one who gets my blood pressure up."

"I'm just saying…consider it a gift. Cherish every moment.

Goodbye, sir."

As Steve walked out of the room, the chief chuckled to himself and sat back down to his regular hectic day.

* * *

The bartender at the Broken Clock Tavern topped off another pitcher of beer and set it on the tray for the waitress to carry to the long haphazard table assembled from all of the individual tables the bar had available. There were thirty detectives and officers drinking and talking at the tables, more at the booths, and some at the bar, all celebrating Steve Bailey's early retirement.

Steve was placed mid-table with Kurt and his dad to one side of him, Rudy and their family to the other side.

Just as Steve was about to take a sip of his beer, he noticed something from the corner of his eye. He put his beer down and told everyone to be quiet.

"Andy, turn that up, would you?"

"Sure thing."

"...We're still amazed by this turn of events. The publicly traded company Mendez MicroTech, which had been seeing all-time highs in the market for months, has taken a steep decline when it was found out that the CEO of the company might have been involved in the security attack against the credit card point-of-sale systems. Levi Mendez has been unavailable for questioning, but he is being searched for by local police and FBI in a joint task effort. In related news, removal of the MicroTech implants is considered a top priority. If you have an implant, please make your way to the nearest clinic, hospital, or doctor's office for safe removal of the device. Do not attempt to remove it yourself. This is Mark Kelly signing off on

KISU News."

"Hey, Tim, how's your hand feeling?" yelled Steve.

Tim lifted his bandaged hand and gave a snarky face back.

"Yeah, sometimes progress hurts," said Steve.

Tim turned his lifted hand to flip the middle finger, then realized Kurt was sitting nearby and quickly pulled his hand under the table, wincing as he bumped it on the edge.

After a look from Kurt's dad, Steve knew it was time for them to get going. Steve asked if they would wait just one moment.

"Hey, everyone, Jim and Kurt have to get going. I'm going to walk them out, but I'll be back in a few minutes."

The trio exited the building and started walking to the parking lot.

"I really wanted to say a few things to you, Kurt, but not in front of all the guys," Steve began. "Would you be so kind as to deliver us to my house momentarily? I'll leave a coin here."

With a blink, they were in Steve's home, sitting down at the table to talk.

"Look," Steve began on a serious note, "I don't have any family. When my wife and son passed, I had no one left to leave anything. I only had my job and my responsibility to the Stone to carry on."

He put his hands on the table as if to steady himself. "The police life is no longer the direction I want to go. It's too limiting in the good that I believe this Stone was meant to do. I'm not sure what that entails, but it's my responsibility to figure that out. I'm going to be leaving the area for a while, and I need someone to look after my things. I don't trust anyone as much as I trust you. It would be an honor if you'd consider my properties as yours."

Kurt's eyes widened, "The cabin, too?"

"Yes, the cabin, too. I've drawn up a power of attorney form which puts your dad in charge of these properties until you reach eighteen years old, and then they will be yours."

Jim asked, "What are you going to do?"

"I'm not sure. First, I know not everyone will go get the operation to remove the implant. If the danger is there, I've got to track down quite a few people and eliminate the threat of that spreading. After that, who knows?"

"I was thinking," said Kurt, "you might not be one hundred percent invincible with that Stone."

"Oh, yeah? How's that?"

"Ever seen the movie *The Highlander*?"

Steve laughed, "OK, you learned my secret. Yes, it's written early in the lore book about that weakness for my Stone, but we generally don't give our secrets out. I promise I'll take care not to lose my head."

Steve went to a drawer and pulled out a ring of various keys, all individually marked. "These are the keys for the locations, although Kurt doesn't generally need keys to get places." He placed them back in the drawer. "I'll let you know when I'm leaving. It's a good idea not to have multiple Stones in the same location, also. Imagine what could happen if a demon were to get a hold of all of them at the same time?"

"We'd have nothing to defend," suggested Kurt. "Yikes. Well, no one is getting my Stone."

"Good, now take me back to the party, I have one other thing for you. Your dad needs to stay here."

Jim had a questioning look on his face but sat down.

Kurt shrugged and transported them back to the parking lot.

Steve stooped down to pick up the coin he lodged under his tire and looked at it.

"You know, we made these to be very unique so you would be able to hone in on them."

"Yeah, like an address, because Gabriel was the Messenger," said Kurt.

"Think about it. You've always been trying to get to places or locations, but if Gabriel was a Messenger, what if your talent is supposed to be to get to people?"

"Whoa, I never thought about that," said Kurt.

He vanished.

Seconds later, he reappeared.

"Oh, that was so easy!"

"I thought it might be," said Steve. "Every person is unique and an easy marker for your Stone to find. Now, think about the opportunities—missing children, hostage situations. You will have quite a bit to think about in the future."

"Wow, that's awesome! I think I want to be a cop like you."

"Look, you'll oversee San Diego now when I'm gone. I'll have my cell phone with me if things get to be too hairy, but you're another Stone holder now, and I'm sure you will be able to handle things brilliantly."

Kurt gave Steve a hug. Steve held back tears. This kid had become so much of a son to him in a short time. He ruffled Kurt's hair, "Be good, kid."

Kurt smiled and disappeared. Tomorrow, Steve knew he would need to start tracking down the rebels with ticking bio-bombs in their hands...and after that, he'd have to find a new place in his family's long history of healers.

But tonight, he could celebrate with friends. Steve turned around and walked back to his retirement party..

THE END

CPSIA information can be obtained
at www.ICGtesting.com
Printed in the USA
FSHW021651010620
70616FS